WATER
AND
BLOOD

SEER SAGA BOOK ONE

INK PLOT PRESS

ISBN 978-1-7330198-2-8
Ebook ISBN 978-1-7330198-3-5

Published by Ink Plot Press LLC
19580 West Indian School Rd, Ste 105
Buckeye, AZ 85396
inkplotpress@kimwilkes.com

Cover Design by Miblart
Author Photo by Madelynn McCombs

kjwilkes.com
inkplotpress.com

For Jason,
You showed me what love is.
And that I deserve it.
I love you.

"People talk about premonition as if it's something strange. It's not. It's just remembering in the wrong direction."

-*Doctor Who, Season 9 Episode 6,*
"The Girl Who Died"

ONE

BLOOD PULSES UNDER MY skin, each heartbeat a stab wound.

Stupid hangnail.

The stabs come faster as my frustration grows. My feet stomp through the undergrowth, keeping time with the pain. Green pine needles brush against me, their trees towering overhead, obscuring the gray sky above.

Erebus wants to help you, Sariah. I cannot understand why you refuse to take him up on his offer. My mother's voice echoes in my head. She bombarded me again this morning as soon as I walked into the kitchen. *Your job is not good for you, honey. Working so many hours is making you sick with stress. A role with the commissioner would be so much more manageable.*

My foot catches on an exposed root and sends the rest of me sprawling forward. I catch myself on a branch, the bark biting into my palm, but I keep my feet.

One breath. In. Out.

The aroma of damp earth and crisp pine fills my nose, calming me. This is why I came here. The forest that surrounds New Harper is the only place I can find true quiet. Where I don't have to put on an act. It's difficult to get out here often enough, mostly because I need my mother's car to do so, but today it was more than necessary.

Because she's right. I'm stretching myself paper thin, and I know it. Sleep is so scarce that my concealer barely hides the deep purple that's bloomed under my eyes. But I don't care. Working for Marshall is the first thing in my twenty-five years of life that feels like mine.

Would a job with the town's commissioner pay more? Of course. But anything from him would come at a cost I'm tired of paying. I've managed to avoid Erebus Copeland for almost a year, and I plan to stay as far away from him as possible. I shake the image of his hard, cold eyes from my mind with a shiver.

But my mother can't understand why I refuse to entertain the offer. Surely she doesn't know what he's done to me. And I've been assured that telling her would wreak horrible consequences. So here we are, stuck in this dance of frustration. The same fight plays out over and over again. Our conversations have grown increasingly one-sided. But that's my fault. I'm pulling away. My last doctor said that can happen with resentment. Of course, then I had to set him straight. Explain how I don't resent Audrey Invidia, how I could never feel malice towards the woman who raised me.

Not when she reads every one of my reports.

She insists her close watch is only to track my progress. She was my first doctor, after all. Before I requested to meet with someone else. But I see the way she looks at the commissioner. And I know all too well the way he looks at me.

The soft trickle of water fills the air as I step into the small clearing. My shoulders fall.

One breath. In. Out.

I drop my bag next to a downed tree trunk that sits beside the stream. The water is clear in the overcast light, gliding over small stones and sparse blades of grass. I raise my hands overhead to stretch, the folds of my large black hoodie bunching around my neck. My breath fogs in the morning air. Dropping my arms, I step over the log and sit. I just need a moment to close my eyes. I'll feel better after a minute.

Hunched over my knees, I run my hands down my face, careful to avoid smudging my eyeliner. I have a shift after this. I picked it up before leaving work late last night. Honestly, it surprised me that my mother was home to talk to me at all. I was sure I'd be gone before she woke up. But it turns out she entertained the urge to search my room while I was away, and she found papers from the apartment complex on the other side of town.

Be serious, Sariah, she'd said, brandishing the folder. *There is no reason for it. The best thing for you is to stay here with me. So, drop it.*

That was it. End of conversation. And I couldn't argue. As much as I want my own space, this town isn't big enough to hide in. Moving out wouldn't be an escape, not really. So why even bother?

A sigh pushes out of my throat, and I register the sting in my palm. When I turn it over in my lap, I see the tiny spots of blood bulging from the scrape. I scoot down from the log onto the bank, crouching so I can lean forward and reach the stream to rinse it. The idea loops through my mind: Escape.

As my fingers break the surface of the chilled water, something rustles in the branches behind me. I spin to spot the source of the sound, but the motion sends me slipping over the edge of the bank. My hand splays out to brace my fall as the water rushes up to meet me. A sharp rock digs into my palm, the searing pain instant, and so much worse than the small scrape. The scream wrenches itself from my mouth.

Rather than crashing into the rocky bed of the stream, I feel my body rip apart deep in my abdomen. The air is sucked from all around me like a vacuum, silencing my scream and causing my lungs to burn in protest for a split second before soft earth smashes against my face. My forehead throbs from the impact. I roll myself over, clutch my wounded hand to my stomach, which appears to be intact, and note the water that seeps into my shoes.

That's not right.

My hand landed in the stream, not my feet. I force my eyes open. Glimpses of light shine in the pockets of sky visible through the treetops. The tree cover is too dense. These woods are too dark. How hard did I hit my head? I push up into a seated position and pull my soggy feet from the water, still trying to piece together how I could have fallen so far forward.

A laugh sounds in the distance, a musical soprano trill. It dawns on me that I'm exposed, and I cast my eyes around for a hiding place. A large tree directly behind me offers cover, so I scoot back to claim its shadow.

Light footsteps charge past in rapid succession.

"Come on, Vanessa, keep up!" A girl's voice calls out as she runs past the other side of the tree. I turn myself as quietly as possible so that my chest rests against its bark, and I slowly lean out to catch a glimpse of whoever may be approaching. My hands grip the rough bark for balance, the cut in my palm protesting. A young girl in a white dress comes barreling through the forest, her sneakers slapping the earth. She stops only a stone's throw from where I hide to rest her hands against her knees, gulping at the air. She's young, her face still round and smooth. Dark hair hangs loose down her back. I shift slightly for a better view, and a small twig snaps beneath my foot.

Blue eyes dart to the sound, but I duck back, clinging to the tree, not breathing.

"Vanessa, hurry up!" The other voice cries out, farther away now. After a moment, the girl takes off again, the sound of her feet disappearing into the thick expanse of unfamiliar woods.

My breath returns to me, though shaky. I dreamt this only a few hours ago. I woke in a cold sweat. It's the only reason I was up so early after the long night.

But this... this is not a dream.

My body shakes. I pull the sleeves of my hoodie down over my hands, a shield from this strange place, flinching when I hit my wounded hand. Liquid oozes out of my palm. It's dark in the shadow of the tree, but I recognize the coppery stench as blood, nearly collapsing at the sight of it smeared across my hand and fingers, coating the exposed skin. It's dark and wet and my frenzied brain screams at me to get it off.

Whipping my head back and forth, I check for any other sound, any other movement in the branches, but there is none.

My breath is too shallow, too fast. I crawl forward on my knees, holding the wound aloft, shuffling towards the large river that has taken the place of the slow stream. I have to get out of here. I have to get back home. I thrust my hand into the water so that it will rip away the disturbing blood.

A force pulls deep in my gut, like gravity has latched onto my insides, and I'm yanked backwards.

Before I can blink, everything around me changes. White, hazy sunlight fills the clearing, the rush of water once again a lazy trickle.

I'm back. Water drips from the fingertips I still hold out in front of me, the angry red line in my skin clearer now, no longer oozing. It burns like fire.

I stand, but my legs are jelly, and they falter. I rest my weight again on the fallen trunk.

One breath. In. Out.

Run. I have to get out of here. This place isn't safe after all.

I fish in my bag with my good hand and pull out the keys, grateful they're still there. Steeling myself, I rise slowly. Once I find my footing, I break into a stilted trot back down the trail, not stopping until the car door handle is in my grip. Inside, my hand fumbles to pull the door shut. It takes two tries to get the key in the ignition, then I rev the engine, peeling backwards onto the road toward town.

These familiar trees flit past the windows like apparitions. I'm driving too fast. I need to get myself under control. The clock tells me it's only been two hours since I left home.

I'll be early for work, but Marshall won't mind. I can clean myself up, wait in the break room, and get my head right.

Once I pull back into town, I force the car to slow. My breath hisses through my teeth. That water should have been clean, so why does the cut burn?

When I turn the corner, I see the parking lot of the convenience store is busy. Though anything seems busy compared to its almost deserted state during the late shift. I tuck the borrowed car between a set of painted white lines and turn it off.

Get the first-aid kit. I need to wrap up my hand. That's all. It's no big deal.

I recall the cold sensation of my body being ripped into the dark, unfamiliar forest and shiver. Don't think about that. Think about the fact that your hand is going to get infected if you don't clean it out, Sariah. I grab my bag and force myself out of the car before I can think about it anymore. I tuck my chin as deep into my collar as I can manage, eyes on my damp shoes. My blonde hair hangs around my shoulders in a tangled mess.

Inside is a bustle of cash registers and squeaky cart wheels. I keep to the outer edges of the store and circle around to the back. Two short knocks on Marshall's office.

"Come in." He calls. I tuck my bad hand behind my back, so he doesn't see it, then I go in. "Oh, hey there, Sariah. You're here early. Everything okay?" He pushes back from his desk and the litter of paperwork covering it.

"Yeah, of course." I lie. "I just wondered if I could grab the first-aid kit?" I thought he'd be home sleeping. He's been working nights too.

"Sure. Why? Are you hurt?" He grabs the white plastic box from the wall and holds it out to me. I reach for it with both hands, exposing the ugly cut but remembering too late. Marshall notices. "That looks pretty nasty." He says.

"It's nothing. I'll just go to the restroom and take care of it." I take the box by its handle and retreat a step.

"Sariah, wait." Marshall gestures to a chair in front of his desk. Defeated, I take a seat. "Look kid, I know it's not my business, but I've been worried about you. You're a great employee, don't get me wrong. But it seems like something is bothering you. And if you're walking in here bloodied up, I can't in good conscience look the other way." He stares me down with his kind eyes.

I swallow past the tightness in my throat and hold out my hand. "I was hiking." My voice is small, but he nods his head, his mouth pressed into a hard line.

"You know the woods are restricted, Sariah. They're dangerous. You shouldn't be out there at all, and especially not alone." He leans in a little closer to inspect the cut, though the squirm of his tight lips and the sheen forming on his forehead make it clear he'd rather not.

I take my hand back. "I can handle it, Marshall. I'll go clean this up."

"This doesn't have anything to do with the commissioner, does it? I've been getting some calls." He clears his throat. "I want you to know, you have a place here. If you want it. Or if you need it." He leans back, staring me down again.

A lump forms in my throat. I blink away invading tears.

"Thank you." I stand and make it to the door before turning around. "Please don't report this." My eyebrows pull together. I know I probably don't need to make the request of him, but I really do not want Copeland to have this as another reason in his arsenal to convince everyone I should be working for him instead.

Marshall folds his arms over his chest and answers. "Okay."

TWO

THE SCANNERS ON THE cash registers beep. Drawers clang open and shut, and packs of gum crinkle against paper bags while the bell on the front door dings. The morning shift was uneventful. Rather than going home, I convinced Marshall to let me work through the evening. He argued I should get some rest, but he could see my desperation and ultimately relented.

The customer at my station collects his receipt, and then my manager calls me on the hand radio. "Sariah, I'm going to leave Jodie on register one. Lock yours up for now, then I need you to restock shelves." I look up and see him in an aisle. He shoves a thumb over his shoulder toward a cart of boxes.

"Sure thing." I say, turning to the register and locking it. I adjust the bandage wrapped around my bad hand, making sure the cut stays covered.

The cart holds boxes of toilet paper, granola bars, and a small shipment of alcohol. I push it towards the refrigerators in the back to shelve the drinks first, one of the wheels sticking. But when I round the corner, a group of guys stands perusing the beer. I recognize one of them in particular.

Not again.

They laugh and shove at each other. I duck into the next aisle before they see me, crouching behind the cart, and start putting the toilet paper rolls on a bottom shelf. I hate it when they come here.

Vomit teases at the back of my throat, and I take a deep breath through my nose to force it down.

One breath. In. Out.

I can avoid them this time. Charles won't even know I'm here if I can lie low.

As I stack a roll in its place, dirt-caked boots appear a few paces to my right. In my periphery, their owner reaches for a bar of soap. He's tall with tousled brown hair, and soft shadows under his eyes that hint at stress, though he can't be much older than I am. I must not have a monopoly on sleepless nights. His dark pants are worn, as is the flannel peeking out from under his jacket. I know most of our regular shoppers, but I can't place him. While I'm staring, our eyes meet. His are blue, and they widen with apparent recognition, then with shock.

Strange. I duck my head, heat rushing to my cheeks.

"Hey there!" I jump and turn to find one of the other guys leaning on my cart. Charles. I curse under my breath. He picks up a glass neck from the cart, spinning it around lazily. "I see you've got a few bottles here. Think you could hook me and my friends up with a drink? We haven't found what we're looking for in the fridge." The way his gaze rakes down my uniform shows the double meaning in his words.

I pull my hair around my shoulder with one hand, letting the blonde curtain create enough separation for me to steel myself.

The frayed ends are brittle against my pulsing fingertip, the hangnail still angry as ever. I grab the box of booze and shoulder my way to the fridge door. I won't jeopardize this job, even if these particular customers are awful. Charles works at the government offices, doing something or other for Commissioner Copeland. I'm not sure where he picks up the rest of his friends, but he clearly has poor taste. The group surrounds me with wolfish grins, the cold seeping under my sleeves as I hurry to empty the box. When I turn to walk away, the men are closer than I realized. I take a step forward, but they don't let me pass. One whispers something, and the others chuckle. My breath quickens, eyes darting between each of their faces.

They wouldn't be dumb enough to pull something here, would they? Not with Marshall in the back. Logically, I'm in a safe place. I could call out for help, and someone would probably come. But as I look between each sneering face, dizziness takes over my vision, and I can barely suck air into my lungs to keep from passing out.

"Is there a problem here?" I grip the fridge door, steadying myself enough to comprehend it's the man from the aisle speaking. His half-filled shopping basket lies abandoned on the scuffed-up white tiles of the floor. His hands hang loose and ready at his sides, shoulders drawn up and back. He's tall, markedly taller than any of the men surrounding me.

Charles turns his head, lips pulling downward into a scowl. "You can move along." His eyes squint in warning.

The man jerks his chin at me. "I think it's time you let her get back to her job."

Charles barks a single laugh. "What are you, her boyfriend?"

He doesn't reply. He also doesn't move.

I'm a statue, my feet frozen to their spot, half in and half out of the fridge. Frigid air snakes inside my shirt collar to caress my spine.

The muscle in Charles's jaw ticks in agitation. He takes a step towards the intruder. "Mind your own business. Get out of here before my friends teach you a lesson."

Those striking blue eyes size up the group of opponents. "How about you all mind your own business and leave her alone?"

The men around me stir. One of them nudges Charles. "Let's get rid of this guy."

Charles huffs a breath. "Fine, we'll leave her alone. If you come with us out back."

He meets my gaze, searching for something. I don't budge an inch. After a beat, he replies. "Okay."

The group laughs again, passing around their wicked glee. They file out of the store.

He looks at me one more time, then ducks his head and follows them.

Once I lose sight of them through the windows, the blood returns to my toes, and I drop the empty cardboard box. I shove past the cart in the aisle and rush to Marshall's office. My manager isn't here. I tiptoe to the green door that leads to the back alley. Quiet. Be quiet. I press my ear against the chilled metal. The smack of skin on skin makes me jump.

One breath. In. Out.

I should get Marshall.

But first, I need to see what I'm sending him out to face.

Crouching, I push the door open the tiniest sliver. The group surrounds their leader and the stranger. Charles is throwing punches. The man takes each hit. One slams his face and sends him staggering back. He wipes a dribble of blood from the corner of his mouth.

"Done yet?" he deadpans.

At the same time, another from the group comes at him from behind, aiming an elbow toward his ribs. He detects the move out of the corner of his eye and spins to throw him off balance, pushing the attacker's back so that he barrels into Charles. If they were having fun before, now they are angry. They are seriously going to hurt him.

I let the door whisper shut and run back to the main floor, craning my neck over the aisles. I need to find Marshall immediately. The moment of searching stretches for an eternity, but then I find him. "Marshall!" I wave at him frantically. He sets his clipboard on a shelf and follows me.

"What's the matter?" He takes in my panic.

"There's a fight in the alley. An entire group is going after one guy. We need to help him."

Marshall nods and pushes past me, speeding through the hall straight for the door.

He's a big guy, not especially tall, but with a round belly, giant shoulders, and arms like tree trunks. Because this is common knowledge, this store experiences fewer robberies than all the others in town.

I trail him, stopping short at the back door as he marches into the dim alley.

"This is a professional establishment. I will not tolerate any violence around my store. You lot clear out." He hollers.

The men scatter, curses on their breath. Meanwhile, I note with sick satisfaction that Charles is sprinting with a limp.

But that feeling falters as soon as the fray clears and I see one body crumpled on the ground.

THREE

MY HANDS SHAKE, AND I can't push my feet beyond the safety of the building, so I watch from the doorway. The white of the overhead lights oozes around my shadow onto the pavement, casting a menacing stain that dies before reaching the men. The sun has set, making them appear as outlines against the dark of the alleyway. Marshall kneels to turn the body over. His shoulders sag as he bows his head, then he readjusts and reaches under both arms to heave the man up. He drags him towards the store, and I pull the door open wider to make room.

Marshall trips over the doorframe, and the man slips from one of his arms. I lunge to upright him, struggling. My boss nods towards his rolling desk chair. I wrap my arms around the man's bicep so I don't drop him and start side-stepping to the seat. He smells like pine and fresh cotton. And another scent drifts off him. Metallic. We count to three and lower him into the chair as gently as we can mange. Marshall is more controlled than I am, my muscles screaming under the weight. I drop him more than lower him, and his head snaps sideways with the fall.

"Oops." I press my hands against his shoulder to keep him from toppling onto me. The jolt wakes him up, and he blinks against the light. If his hair was tousled before, it's completely disheveled now, hanging over his forehead. Why did he agree to follow Charles out there?

Marshall's walkie-talkie crackles to life at his belt.

"Marshall, we've got a customer complaint at register one, can you come up here?" It's Jodie. We keep only two radios in the store. One by the registers and one for Marshall. It's quicker than sending someone to find him when there is an issue up front.

He unclips the black rectangle from his waist and holds down the red button. "Copy." He replaces it and looks at me. "Can you take care of this, Sariah? You know where the medkit is. Hopefully, this will just take a minute. I'll come back to file the report." My eyes widen, but I nod. The least I can do is help clean the wounds this man sustained for my sake.

The stranger gives his head little shakes, still trying to return to the present. Marshall leaves, and the door whispers shut behind him. I'm suddenly aware of exactly how small this office is. I study the man in the chair. Could it be that his behavior had nothing to do with me? He might have been searching for a thrill, picking a fight for fun. That option would be more logical. And now we're here alone. The thought spikes my heart rate.

One breath. In. Out.

I go to the wall to pull down the white plastic box of medical supplies that I replaced here this morning. Glancing over my shoulder, I eye the man from behind. The skin of his neck is tanned, dotted with faint freckles, and his brown leather jacket hugs his shoulders. I chide myself for being so anxious.

This guy just stood up for me. More than that, he got himself hurt in my defense. If he had wanted to use me, he wouldn't have done that.

Right?

Still, I walk the wider route, circling around the front of the desk to stand by him again. I spread the kit open on top of the disarray of multicolored papers. The contents are sparse, mostly small adhesive bandages.

One breath. In. Out.

"Um, are you okay?" I peek at his face from under my lashes.

He grips his chin with long fingers, rubbing at a sore spot. His eyes focus on me, and the corner of his mouth hitches up before he grimaces in pain. "Yeah, I'm okay." He takes his fingers from his mouth, and they shine bright red.

My hands shoot for the gauze pads, ripping a few open and handing them to him. He takes them and presses one inside his cheek. I search his face as he uses the rest to wipe the blood. He's got a cut on his temple that is also dripping. I open more gauze. My fingers tense around it, and it takes all my willpower to push my arm forward and to press the gauze to his head. The touch makes his eyes flick up at me. Clear blue, like water deep enough to drown in.

"Thank you." He mumbles softly around the wad of fabric.

My lips spread into a tight closed smile. "I should thank you. You didn't have to do that. With all those guys." I say.

The white turns crimson between my fingers. I drag the wastebasket from under the desk to discard the soiled gauze. With less bleeding, the dirt in his gash is visible.

Alcohol wipes, where are the alcohol wipes?

"Yes, I did. You don't deserve to put up with that." He says. His eyes are still on me. I look anywhere else. The supplies clutter the desk now, and there are no alcohol wipes.

I sigh. "Can you scoot over a bit? I need to open that drawer." I point to the bottom right drawer of the desk. He pushes the chair aside, but the gap between him and the desk is still small enough to make me hold my breath. I fumble it open and pull out one of the bottles Marshall hides inside. I open another packet of gauze and carefully wet it with the clear liquid. "This might sting." I warn him, pressing it to the wound. His sharp intake of breath confirms my assumption. "Sorry." I mutter.

He squeezes his eyes shut and breathes through his nose.

"How would you know what I deserve?" The question escapes my mouth before I can stop it, and I immediately wish I could reel it back in.

He opens his eyes and answers without hesitation. "You deserve to feel safe, Sariah."

"How did you...?" I remember the name tag attached to my shirt, glance down to confirm it's there. Of course.

His cheeks flush. He clears his throat. "Is there somewhere I can wash up?" He holds his palms up towards me. Smeared with blood.

"Yeah, there's a restroom around the corner." I nod toward the door.

He stands, but wavers. He grips the edge of the desk to balance. I should offer to help him, let him lean on me so he doesn't fall over, but I stand back and watch instead. He steadies, then proceeds toward the doorway. Looking back at me, he points, confirming the direction he's supposed to go. I nod.

Then he's gone.

I feel the tremors starting in my lower back. No. Not now.

One breath. In. Out.

Control it.

I distract myself by tidying up the desk and returning the kit to its place on the wall. Marshall lumbers back in. He looks around.

"Where did he go?"

"To the restroom."

"I just came from the restroom." He looks at me puzzled.

We both leave the office and round the corner. Sure enough, the restroom is empty.

"He said he wanted to wash his hands." Why would he disappear? I messed this up, didn't I?

"It's all right, Sar. Nobody likes paperwork. We both know filing the report wouldn't make much difference." Marshall heaves a sigh before returning to the shop floor.

Reluctantly, I follow. I find the cart I left by the fridge and finish restocking the shelves. Keep my hands busy. Keep moving. When I start to wheel the empty cart forward, it skids to a halt, caught on something. A shopping basket half filled with soap, toothpaste, and food. What was the man's name? Did I ask him?

A hole opens in the pit of my stomach. Something about this whole night feels wrong.

FOUR

MORE BLOOD.

Mine this time.

Of course it would happen now. I'm careful to keep things clean, pulling the slightly stained underwear back up my legs. Luckily, I haven't bled through my pants yet. I wash my hands and hurry to the health aisle to find my usual. It's on the top shelf.

The label reads:

NEW HARPER MANUFACTURING

FEMININE PADS

ZERO LEAKS

—— GREAT ABSORBANCY ——

VERY SECURE

New Harper Manufacturing

Feminine Pads
Zero Leaks
Great Absorbency
Very Secure

So many promises for a little napkin meant to soak up my monthly bleed. I pluck up the first box ready to rush back to the restroom, but something green flutters to the white tile below. I stoop down to retrieve it. Rectangular holes mar the flat card, six of them placed randomly across the paper. I check the shelf and shift some other boxes around. Nothing else hiding there. This card wasn't here the last time I stocked these pads, was it? Not that I can recall. I flip the card and see a string of numbers scrawled across the bottom. Six sets of numbers.

That's odd.

Coincidence or connection?

Six squares, six numbers. My brain can't help but cling to the suggestion of a puzzle. A trained tendency. For as long as I can remember, my mother and the string of doctors following her have prescribed me logic books to work on. Said they would help my brain, help the anxiety, whatever. They never helped much, if at all, but I became pretty adept at puzzles. I flip the card twice more, looking over every inch of the green paper.

Six hollow rectangles. Uneven rectangles, some squared, others stretched. And six sets of numbers, written clearly and equidistant from another. Clearly meant to be separate and not one long string.

My heartbeat pounds painfully around my hangnail, vying

for my attention, a sign I'm getting too worked up.

"Everything okay?" It's Marshall again, making his rounds. "I'll be locking up soon."

I nod my head, tucking the card against the box in my other hand. "Yeah, I'm fine. Just need to use the restroom. I'll head home in a minute." He nods and walks off.

I huff a small laugh at myself. What am I doing? Standing around like an idiot because I found a piece of trash?

The indicator on the bathroom door shows green. My coworkers have already clocked out and left.

I flip the lock inside and resume my previous perch on the toilet.

More blood.

I bring the box into view so I can open it. Huh. The green card matches the box's dimensions. I glance at the locked door. This shouldn't take long to solve. Marshall won't leave without checking on me. I have time.

I slide the card against the smooth cardboard of the box, making sure the edges all align perfectly. A smattering of letters peeks through the squared windows.

TU L KS B CY RE

Gibberish. A code?

Or my mistake?

My pulsing finger taps the side of the box. I flip the card horizontally, so the string of numbers is visible in the bottom right corner. New letters appear.

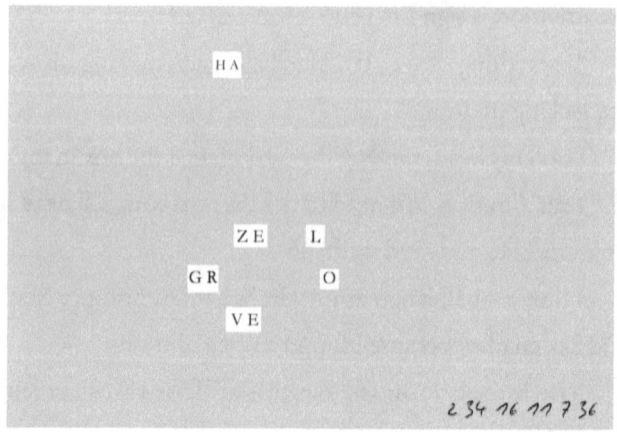

HA ZE L GR O VE

Hazelgrove.

Not a word I know, but certainly a word.

Not a coincidence then.

But what about the numbers?

KNOCK, KNOCK, KNOCK.

I jump at the loud pounding on the door. Three raps in quick succession.

"Hey Sariah, you still in there? I'm about ready to leave." Marshall calls through the wood.

"Sorry, Marshall! I just need a minute." The string of numbers stares up from the card, taunting me, full of secrets to untangle.

"Alright. Would you mind locking up? I've got somewhere I need to be." A quiet clink sounds, then a single gold key shoots across the tile floor towards me. "Sorry to duck out. Get home safe, yeah?"

"No problem, Marshall, I've got it!" It's not the first time he's asked me to close the store. I listen to his heavy soles plod down the hall.

Do I plan to keep sitting on this toilet?

I open the top of the box, careful not to damage the label on the front. Once I've situated myself, I set the box and card on the toilet tank so I can wash my hands. I flip on the sink, but train my eyes on the green slip of paper. Where did it come from? Who would hide puzzles in feminine products? Women in New Harper are ashamed to visit that section of our store, let alone spend extra time there.

With dry hands, I snatch up my things and open the door. The squeak of my shoe explodes into the silence. I take a few more careful steps into the now dimly lit hall, an uneasy feeling crawling up the back of my neck, then break into a run, crashing into Marshall's office. I smash the light switch, turning my back to lean against the wall and catch my breath.

Under the bright humming lights, I shake my head at myself. Stupid. Pull yourself together, Sariah.

I sit at Marshall's cluttered desk and grab one of the many pens strewn across its surface. Then, I slide the green card onto the desk in front of me, my pulse pounding in my ears.

Time to settle these numbers.

2 34 16 11 7 36

Could be a cipher.

The box of pads watches me from its perch on the desk. It must connect to the box, right? The box is the key. Could it be as simple as counting?

Grabbing the box, I count out each letter. I stop at the letter corresponding to each number set and mark it on the card, creating a vertical trail.

E

S

C

A

P

E

A sharp gasp bursts from my lips.

Escape.

I read the word over and over, a magnetic pull blooming in my chest.

Escape.

But why? Why is this here? And what does it mean?

Hazelgrove. Escape.

Nonsense.

The stabbing in my finger starts again, and I pick at the hangnail. That only makes it hurt worse. I huff a breath and move to throw the card in the trash, but stop. Instead, I stuff it in the box and take both to the break room.

My purse sits ready in my locker, and I throw the box inside, double-checking that my keys and wallet are there too. No messages on my phone. Guess my mother turned in early. Or she felt her last words were sufficient.

Time to go home. In the dark.

The hole in my stomach returns, this time accompanied

by the cramping pain I ignored earlier. I should have anticipated my bleed, but this morning was a whirlwind. The intense dream, the fight with my mother, whatever happened in that clearing... I'd nearly pushed the memory from my mind. Now it returns to me full force. Everything together creates a swirling vortex of gravity that threatens to crumple me in on myself.

One breath. In. Out.

I shrug on my dark hoodie over my polo and remove my name tag, leaving it on the locker shelf.

Turn around. Move my feet. Try not to think.

Outside, the night air sinks a million minuscule bites into the exposed skin of my face and hands. I lock the back door, then find the fake brick hidden in the wall. Once I wrestle it out, I slot the key into the hole inside its back and push it into place again. Marshall's way of letting some employees help without creating extra keys. He doesn't need an extra security risk in this town. I pass the store's windows, plastered with the faces of missing persons on black and white posters. The streetlights buzz, illuminating the hard, gray landscape of the street. Old buildings tucked one next to the other, all corners and bricks and cement.

I wait for the late bus in the cold. Again. The bench at the bus stop squats empty and freezing and entirely uninviting. I opt to stand, shuffling my feet and puffing warm air onto my fingers.

Black fills the sky, save for the faint white glow where the moon has come out of hiding. Its growing smile mocks me. I turn my eyes down and open my bag to check for gloves. That's when I notice the keys again. I have my mother's car.

All the distractions made me forget I don't need the bus.

Tires screech around the corner, and my head snaps up in time to see a large black car careen into the empty bus lane. Music blares from the speakers as the car halts in front of me. The windows roll down, and I recognize the men from the store.

They call out to me. "Come on in, sweetheart, we'll help you warm up."

It's not the cold that freezes me now. My whole body turns to ice. Sweat pools in my armpits and in the hair at the nape of my neck, adrenaline flooding my system. Move, Sariah. Move.

I slowly reach a hand down to pull my phone from my pocket. The men continue to bait me. I turn to leave, start dialing Marshall's number, then I hear the car door open. Over my shoulder, I spot two hulking figures jumping from the back seat.

I run. My sneakers slam against the pavement, my purse pounding against my side with every step. The fear drowns out the protests of my legs, and I push as hard as I can, the freezing night air slicing down my throat before ripping back out of my chest and turning to vapor. I will make it to the car. I can lock the doors, so they won't be able to get me. It's not far. I push harder, sending each step as far as it can reach in front of me.

But it's not enough. The men are bigger and faster, taking me over, grabbing me, and picking me up off the ground so I can't move. My phone slips from my stiff fingers and clatters against the cement.

"Leave me alone!" Caught in my ragged throat, the words are barely louder than a whisper.

They haul me to the car and dump me on the backseat. Before I can push away, another set of hands close around my waist. I'm dragged over the leather, the two others piling in after me and slamming the door shut.

FIVE

IT HURTS.

My face hits the dirt hard, and skin peels off where my cheek meets gravel. The men laugh as they drive away. Nothing. They left me with nothing. They took the clothes off my back and replaced them with bruises. Lost, naked, helpless, and bleeding in the rain, I curl up against the cold ground and cry.

Tap. Tap. Tap.

The raindrops are mockingly gentle.

Hair sprawls out from under my head, light against the black pavement. Each strand dims slowly as it takes on water, swallowed by shadow. Pines brush the night sky around me. They must have dumped me on the edge of town, out where no one lives, and I won't be able to find help. I wonder whether my mother would search for me here, or if my face would be pasted up on a new missing persons poster, added to the collection on the store windows. It could be that those faces were dumped here too.

My thoughts spiral to a halt, not wanting to contemplate anymore what happened.

The hole in my stomach swallows the rest of me. I feel nothing now.

I cast my eyes down to see if I'm still there at all. Beads of red roll down my legs, mingling with the water pooling in the crevices between my body and the street.

I wish I could disappear.

For a moment, I think unconsciousness is welcoming me. My sight goes dark, except for a single moonbeam casting light onto the earth near the trees. Two eyes appear in the shadows, luminous and low to the ground. From the foliage emerges a black fox. Light on its feet, it walks closer, ears twitching to follow every whisper of the forest.

My eyes flutter open, and I find myself still stuck to the wet ground. The animal has vanished. It was probably a hallucination. Another dream.

New footsteps approach, soft and quiet. I don't have the energy to tense or try to move. Whatever happens now won't be worse than what I've already been through. Why bother putting up a fight? The figure stops next to me, then warmth falls around me in the form of a flowing piece of fabric.

"Come, child," a woman's voice whispers. It's not what I expected, not in the woods in the middle of the night. Curiosity stirs me enough to follow her prompting.

Soft, strong hands help me off the ground.

I stand on shaking legs and stumble. The woman's arm comes around my shoulders to support me. The moon is still smiling, but it's brighter here. Or I hit my head hard enough to affect my vision. I stare at it, eyes drooping, head lolling. What is happening?

"Who are you?" I ask over my fattened lip.

The woman shushes me, patting my shoulder as she ushers me along, veering into the tree line off the road. My thoughts grow fuzzy. I hold fast to the sides of the blanket that meet at my chest and focus on my toes moving forward, padding over the rocks and sticks in slow progression.

I hear a door open and feel the ground shift to flat wooden floorboards. We are inside a home. She guides me to a long table draped with a white sheet and helps me lie down. I don't resist. It's better than lying on the gravel outside.

Warm light flickers against the slats. Fighting for consciousness, I force my eyes to watch the woman. She pulls items from a cupboard across the room. Panic bubbles in my stomach, though the sensation is distant, as if it's happening to a different version of me, somewhere else. But as I watch the woman's long ebony curls sway against her back, a sense of peace overcomes me.

"Who are you?" I ask again, though the screams stole most of my voice. The woman carries an armful of small canvas bags, matches, and a palm-sized gold bowl back to a table beside my head, her path lit by candles all around the room. Her complexion is dark, as if she spent her whole life basking in the glaring sun, but still soft and unlined. Warm brown eyes crease when she smiles softly.

"I am called Sophia." From her knitted sweater pocket, she retrieves a piece of cloth and begins to blot the dirt and wounds on my face. The pain is excruciating, not distant in the slightest, despite her gentle touch. But the only reaction I can muster is a few tight breaths.

She takes her time cleaning each wound, and eventually my

inhalations grow deeper, taking in the scent of herbs and flowers, bitter and rosy.

Sophia opens one of the bags and pulls out a small black square. A match bursts to life, turning the square red, then white, billowy smoke rising. From another bag she withdraws a small yellow stone, placing it in the bowl with the burning square.

My nose fills with the smoke, the incense wafting me into sleep.

A BLUR OF LIGHT and shadow swallows my surroundings. My hands grip fingers. I step with care, my heart beating out of rhythm.

The hairs on my neck rise, and a stream of light hurdles down in front of me. In the flash, a body falls to the ground.

I WAKE WITH HALF a sob, bolting upright, panic gripping my chest as I take in my surroundings. Daylight hints through the windows of the small cabin.

"Breathe, dear." Sophia sits nearby in a deep armchair with hands folded across her lap. She rises and walks to the table where the incense had been. In its place, a tray with two porcelain cups and a white ceramic teapot waits. She pours both servings and unfolds my hand from the blanket swaddling my body. Turning my palm up, she sets one of the cups in it and wraps my fingers around its warm surface.

A small circular stool rests next to the table, and she sits, sipping on her own cup of yellow and sage hued tea. "Are you going to report them?" She meets my eyes. I hold the cup, deciding whether I should drink.

"What are you talking about?" I don't recall telling the woman anything after she found me.

"I spent the evening dressing your wounds, child. It is clear what they put you through. Will you report the men who did it?" Sophia's voice is even and matter-of-fact.

When I meet her gaze, my defenses break.

I lament, "What's the point? These sorts of things are never taken seriously in New Harper. Besides, it's their word against mine, and there were four of them." My face crumples, the events of the night taking horrible shape in my mind. I don't want to remember.

Sophia's lips turn down, age becoming more prominent in the crease between her brows. "You underestimate yourself," she sighs and lifts herself from the stool. Behind her, an armoire of dark wood sits against the wall. She opens one of the doors and pulls out a blue cotton dress and some fresh-looking undergarments. "You may put these on. Best we get you home before anyone has a chance to worry."

My head snaps to the window. The sky is a pale shade of blue now. I sniff hard and wipe my eyes. She's right. I have to time this correctly. A barrage of questions from my mother would break me right now. Sophia gathers the tray of tea to the sink, her back turned to me. Lacking the patience to question the woman further, I slide from the cot and snatch up the clothes. I pull them on in a rush, trying not to look at any of my skin.

Instinctively, I go for the front door. When my hand grips the handle, it strikes me that I don't know where I am or how to get home. I turn on my heel slowly, taking a moment to notice the old books stacked along shelves and tables. A hearth holds a dying pile of flames. Above the sink in the kitchen, there is a wide window overlooking the forest. Strung above it, dried bundles of leaves and flowers hang upside down.

A melodic hum emanates from Sophia as she returns to the armoire and pulls out two brown shoes from its floor. "I'll guide you back to your home, Sariah." She doesn't even glance at me as she says it.

"How do you know who I am?" I know I haven't shared my name, and the purse with my ID was stolen.

Sophia comes to stand before me and places a gentle hand on my shoulder. She is taller than I am, and I'm forced to lean my head back like a child to meet her gaze. "That is a conversation for another time. Let's get you home." She reaches past me to open the door.

I hurry to slip on the leather shoes she hands to me. They fit. I follow her, feeling bare without any of my own belongings.

"You haven't been sleeping well," she states once I catch up to walk by her side.

I stiffen. "Have I been here more than one night?" It occurs to me I could have slept longer than I thought. Are there lapses in my memory?

"No, you rested only a few hours. I am referring to the dreams." She moves through the trees without a branch brushing her, like this forest was custom-fit to her shape. "I'm afraid this season may not hold much rest for you," Sophia sighs. She walks with purpose but does not hurry.

Dread seeps into my pores. No one outside of my doctors is meant to know about the dreams. Well, my doctors and Commissioner Copeland. No one is supposed to live in these woods either.

The trees clear onto the main road, where she found me. A white sedan pulls up, and she opens the back door.

Who is this baffling woman?

"I am sorry I cannot go with you. John will take you home. I understand this is difficult for you, but I promise you can trust him."

My whole body seizes with trepidation. Another car with another man. A vise of fear squeezes the base of my spine.

But I have no alternative way home. If I don't return before my mother wakes up, she will have questions. She'll call Copeland. She'll force me to tell her what happened, and I don't want to do that. It is just the ammunition she needs to make sure I take the internship. I have to hope she assumes I've been sleeping, but oh. Oh, no. The car. If the car's not there when she leaves for work, she'll know I'm gone.

One breath. In. Out.

I still can't get my feet to move towards the sedan.

Sophia watches me. The driver's door opens, and John climbs out, turning to face me.

I shrink back, my shoulders caving forward.

His lips press into a line, then he walks around the back of the car to stand next to Sophia. He rests his hands on his hips, his chest expanding with a long inhale. He looks to be middle-aged, with dark hair and brown eyes. He wears a driving cap, as well as a gray cardigan over a dark navy buttoned shirt.

On his exhale, he addresses me. "You look like you could use some help."

The words stir a memory. I can't quite pinpoint it, but my shoulders relax.

"I'm sorry we couldn't meet under happier circumstances. But I hope you'll allow me to get you home safely." He reaches a hand up to scratch behind his ear. Marshall does the same thing sometimes. Something loosens in my chest. I take a deep breath. Then nod.

He nods back and retreats to the driver's seat.

I glance at Sophia.

"Truly," she says, "you can trust him."

I steel myself, still feeling naked and empty and raw, and I climb in. Once the seatbelt is secure, I fold my hands in my lap.

Sophia leans into the open passenger seat window. "Thank you, John."

"Yes, ma'am." He nods before facing the wheel and shifting the vehicle into gear.

She turns and walks into the cover of the trees, leaving me

alone with the driver. I don't ask how he knows where to take me. I doubt I'd get a straight answer. My head feels fuzzy, but I need to think. I need to make a plan.

It's early. My mother shouldn't be awake yet. We have to move fast, so she doesn't see me in a strange car.

The hangnail I've managed to claw open stirs as my heart races.

"I don't have my keys." I speak. I don't have any of my belongings. How will I get inside the house?

"We've taken care of that." John leans over to the passenger seat and retrieves my purse, covered in a thin layer of dirt. He extends it back to me, keeping his eyes forward. "Sophia asked me to check the road. It was all on the ground near where she found you."

I take it from him and open it to check the contents. Everything here, though I notice the cash from my wallet is gone. As is my phone. I recall dropping the phone at the bus stop. But the box of pads rests alongside the green card.

Suspicious.

All of it.

I position myself closer to the door, straining against the seatbelt, the pain in my lower back twisting.

I can't fall apart, not yet.

"Can you take me to the convenience store in town? My car is there." I tell the driver.

He glances at me in the rearview mirror. "I hope you'll forgive me, Miss. I took the liberty of returning it to your home. Sophia thought it best that you not drive until you've had more rest."

I open my mouth, then close it again. Who are these people? I settle back into the seat, questions brewing in my mind.

The trees recede the farther we drive, and soon we arrive at the town's familiar streets. I sneak a peek at the dash. The clock has blue-lit numbers: 6:03 a.m. In ten minutes I'll be home.

Provided Sophia and John can be trusted.

My empty stomach turns.

I sit silently, focusing on the time ticking down and the yellow lines on the road.

My mother usually sleeps until seven. I should have a few moments to myself before she's out of bed. But that's only a guess. More of a wish if I'm honest.

6:13 a.m. The car pulls up outside my house, and John shifts it into park. My mother's car sits in the driveway. The garage is closed. She may still be asleep.

One breath. In. Out.

My arms shake, but I force myself to address John. "Thank you. For helping me."

"Of course." He says the words sincerely, and tips his hat to me with a polite, close-mouthed smile. I incline my head before exiting the car, then rush to the side door.

When I unlock it and push it open, the hollow echo of the garage frays my weary nerves. Every sound I make is a risk. A shaky sigh pours out of me, and I quickly close and lock the door, crossing the dark expanse to enter the house.

I tiptoe into my room and rip the brown shoes from my feet along with the clothes Sophia gave me, then stuff them into the back of my closet. I stop at my door to listen for five seconds. No sounds of my mother stirring.

One breath. In. Out.

I don't dare look at my skin. With eyes squeezed shut, I stumble into the bathroom across the hall. I twist the lock and start the shower, not looking towards the mirror. My fingers tremble under the stream of water as I wait for it to turn hot. Climbing in, I pull the curtain closed as quietly as I can manage, then let the heat pour down my back, bracing myself against the wall with my arms.

I sink to the floor, hugging my knees while the jet of hot water pounds my spine. A sob breaks loose, then another, finally cascading out of me, my control broken.

When the water turns cold, I shut it off.

One breath. In. Out.

I stand and use a stale towel to brush the tears from my cheeks, clenching it in my fists. Finally, my breathing slows. I return to my room to get dressed. From my closet, I pull out a long-sleeved shirt and black jeans and slide them onto my body. Thankfully, it's still cold enough to wear one of my large sweatshirts without raising suspicion. My damp hair will drip all over the hood, but I don't care.

I turn to the clock beside my bed. 6:48 a.m.

Six

7:00 A.M.

I sit at the kitchen counter with a bowl of cereal. Exhausted as I feel, the idea of sleep terrifies me. Though more so the dreaming than the sleep. I zero in on the grainy texture of the pieces on my spoon to keep from spiraling, so many questions fighting to enter my stream of consciousness.

A door opens and shuts down the hall, and footsteps approach the kitchen.

My mother walks in and startles when she sees me. "Sariah, you're already up? I was sure you would sleep in after your late shift last night. Which I believe was your third this week if I'm not mistaken." She raises a reprimanding eyebrow at me, then huffs, turning to the cupboard. "I wanted to surprise you. I walked over yesterday and picked these up." She sighs and turns back towards me, looking down at the large donut box in her hands. "Oh, well, surprise, honey." She pushes the box toward me.

I push the lid open, and a half-dozen maple and chocolate glazed doughnuts glitter up at me, though I notice a few bites missing from one. "Thanks, Mom." I hope my small smile passes for a smile at all. I take one of the doughnuts and sink my teeth into the sweet, squishy treat. She knows they're my favorite. But in this moment, the pastry turns to ash between my teeth.

"You would not believe the day I had." My mother circles the counter. She uses her hands to check that her blonde hair is secure in her slicked-back bun, then wraps an arm around my shoulder and kisses the top of my head without stopping to look at me. It takes everything in me not to flinch. "I ran into someone at the bakery." Three beats of expectant silence. "Erebus was there." She continues, blowing past my disinterest. "He asked about you."

Of course.

"He wants to discuss the job offer, have a one on one to define the terms. I told him he can call you today, even stop by if he wants, since you don't have to work until the evening." She collects breakfast items from around the kitchen. "Right? You didn't go picking up any other shifts today, did you?" She doesn't stop what she's doing, but her tone is pointed.

"No," I answer defensively. Then my shoulders tense when I remember. "I lost my phone."

She falters. "What do you mean you lost your phone? I can call it right now. I'm sure you just set it down somewhere and forgot." She slides her own phone from her pocket and starts dialing.

"No, Mom. It's gone." I don't want to elaborate.

She shakes her head in irritation and holds the phone up to her ear. Silly Sariah.

A knock at the front door shoots ice into my spine. No need to guess who is here. My gut tells me to run and hide, but there's no time.

My mother rushes to answer the door, and I hear the faint trill of my phone ringing. It's quickly stifled.

Commissioner Erebus Copeland accompanies my beaming mother back into the kitchen. He's a full foot taller than her, precise posture to match the lines of his suit. His light brown hair is combed back from his face in a neat, professional style. Always ready to impress.

One breath. In. Out.

The tiny ridges in the fabric of my sleeve cuff find my fingers, and I run the cuff between them. Back and forth. Back and forth.

One breath. In. Out.

"Hello, Sariah." Commissioner Copeland wears his glistening smile, all straight teeth and charm. "I planned to call before intruding on your home, but something of yours found its way to my desk." He pulls my phone from the breast pocket of his pressed brown suit and slides it across the counter to me. The bottom corner is chipped, but the keys and screen are intact.

"He came all this way to return it himself, isn't that so kind, Sariah?" My mother shoots daggers from her eyes over her own pasted smile, too wide, the edges of her lips ready to tear open.

"Thank you." I mumble without looking up at him. My damp hair hangs loose around my face. Wet spots have formed on the shoulders of my sweatshirt, now growing cold.

Who picked up my phone? One of the men who grabbed me? Or someone watching? No one else would have known it was mine. It's a standard New Harper model, the most basic tier, but identical to most of the phones in town. It requires a four-digit code to unlock, and I never changed the factory-set screensaver. Why deliver it to the commissioner unless it was to communicate something? A job completed, maybe?

"Not to intrude, but it looks like you could use a new one. We'd be happy to set you up with something at my office. You should come by. We can talk more about the internship." His eyes rake over me. Hungry. Why did I look up? My throat turns dry.

"You should go with him now, honey. No point in waiting around." She comes to stand behind me and starts fussing with my hair. Making me more presentable. A lamb to the slaughter, a show of her devotion. Though maybe she doesn't know that. She can't know that. She just wants what is best for me. A job with fewer hours and higher pay, less stress, like she said. The skin of my thumb turns raw against the cuff. My pulse returns to my finger.

"I'm pretty tired, Mom. I could use some more sleep." Don't make me go. Please don't make me go.

"Of course." Copeland says. "You come whenever you're ready. I can be a patient man." He chuckles. He stands straight but relaxed, his shoes polished and glistening even under the kitchen lights. Only a dusting of gray touches his temples. My mother throws a laugh his way, keeping things amiable. But I understand the dark undertones of his words in a way she doesn't.

She's oblivious. That's what I tell myself. Blinded like everyone else.

Erebus Copeland is good at controlling his image. He runs this town with his suave manners and good looks. He is everyone's friend. Always ready to give you what you want.

As long as you give him what he wants in return.

He edges closer, then grips my chin tenderly between his strong fingers. "Oh, dear, that is a nasty scratch. When did this happen?" I carefully lean out of his grasp, finally looking him in the eye. The knowing behind the façade of concern makes the ice in my spine spread through every inch of my body, like the frost creeping over every pane of glass that lines this street.

My mother exclaims, "Oh, Sariah, I didn't see that! What happened?" She pulls the glasses from the chain around her neck onto her nose.

"It's nothing. I tripped. At the bus stop. I'm fine." I stand to wash my bowl, hoping to excuse myself, and trying my best not to make contact as I shoulder around the commissioner. He takes the opportunity to brush his fingers down my back.

The planes of my face freeze into a neutral expression. He doesn't deserve a reaction.

"That is unfortunate. You should have called. I would have sent someone to get you cleaned up. You needn't rely on the bus, Sariah. I'm more than happy to help. Accept the internship, come work at the city offices." More smiling teeth.

"Yes, honey, you should have called him. Remember after your last tumble? We talked about how he can have the medics help you. He's so generous to offer, Sariah. We ought to have that looked at. Erebus, can you call someone now?" Her eyes are wide with hope and admiration.

"No. I'm fine. I'm going to get some rest." I wish I could sprint to my room and bar the door.

"I'll be off." The commissioner says. "Just wanted to check on you. Make sure you are all right. It has been too long since we've seen one another." He drinks me in with his stare for another moment, then nods to my mother. "Audrey, always a pleasure." He lifts her hand to his mouth and presses a light kiss to her knuckle, then pats it twice with his other hand. "I'll let myself out."

She hurries after him to the door, getting in a few final pleasantries before he disappears. The way a monster disappears when the lights turn on.

I waste no time escaping to my room. One more question, one more intrusion, anything more, will send me over the edge. Once in my bed, sleep envelops me instantly.

Seven

The sunlight slipping in through the slats of my window blinds me the moment my eyes open. Aches flood every bone in my body. The white ceiling occupies my vision as the memories of yesterday creep back into my mind and settle their weight on my chest. I turn over, trying to dislodge the discomfort, but my foot kicks my bag and sends its contents toppling onto the carpet.

I must have tossed my purse onto the bed when I came home and forgotten about it. Tears burn in my eyes. I swipe them away. It's stupid to cry over something so small. I haul myself upright and slide onto the floor. My eyes rake over the items, halting on the green card half hidden under the box of pads.

Hazelgrove.

Escape.

A rapping on my door catches my attention. I sweep everything into a pile on the floor and throw my bag over it before standing to answer the door.

"Have you been sleeping this whole time?" My mother's eyebrows draw together, worry lining her forehead.

"Yes." What else would I be doing?

"We need to get you ready to go into town and meet Erebus.

It's nearly afternoon now. You do not want to keep him waiting all day. I really think it's best to get the new job sorted out as soon as possible." She pushes into the room and opens my closet.

My chest tightens — the clothes from Sophia.

I stuffed them deep into my closet, but my mother has never been afraid of pushing boundaries. How would I explain them if she asks questions?

She whips around with something clutched in her hands. "You should wear this." Yellow bursts from her grip in the form of a short-sleeve dress. The skirt brushes mid-calf. The fabric is light and airy, and the neckline falls into a modest scoop. It's one that she bought for me, but that I've never worn. Not my style. At all.

"I'll be freezing." I reply. It's still cold enough out to see my breath.

"Only outside, and you can wear a coat. Erebus keeps his office at an extremely comfortable temperature, and I know he would love you in this dress. This is a job interview. You must make a good impression." She lays it out gently on my bed. "Try it on and let me see." She steps out and waits in the hall, knowing I won't change if she stands watch. She really is trying to make me hurry.

I click the door shut, grinding my teeth.

Next, she'll insist on driving me down there and walking me up to his office herself, like a child being dropped off at school. I must take charge of this situation. I dig around in my closet for thick black tights and a coat. My fingers curl around the hem of my sweatshirt to peel it off, but then my body starts to shake, anticipating the sight of my skin.

Stop it. Just don't look. I remove the armor of my black hoodie and immediately regret it.

One breath. In. Out.

Quickly, I tear off the rest of my clothes and pull on the new outfit. Once the coat is on and my arms covered, I scoop the pile of belongings back into my bag and stuff some leggings and a long-sleeved shirt inside too. Sadly, my hoodie is too big to fit in the purse. I'll have to settle for my coat.

I open the door and do a spin, making sure my mother sees the flash of yellow I've hidden between the other layers. "You're right, I'll leave now. Can I take the car?"

She hesitates, taken aback for a fraction of a second. "I thought I could take you, actually."

"There's no point in you waiting around. I'll just hurry over and get it all sorted." Please don't call my bluff.

I hold my hand out for the keys.

She pulls them from her pocket with a jangle. I can see the wrestle inside her as she places them in my open palm. She knows it's better to let me do what she's asking willingly than to press the point. We've fought about this enough. I'm finally letting her have her way.

When it comes down to it, we're just two pieces on a board, one always nudging the other through assumption, prediction, and manipulation. It's a game I've learned to play well over all the years we've spent together.

I turn and discreetly grab my sneakers before darting into the garage and hitting the button to raise the door.

Once in the car, I rip out of the driveway, turning left because I know she'll be watching me. As soon as I'm on the next street over, I redirect my course away from town and towards the hills. Sleep still grits my eyes. I never get enough sleep anymore. Maybe I've never gotten enough sleep, period.

As the homes disappear and the trees envelop the street, my chest releases slightly. Sinking disgust replaces the adrenaline. This was my safe place. Here on the outskirts of town. And they tried to take that from me, turning it into a dumping ground, filling it with a terrible memory. I wonder if that was intentional. That would explain how Copeland had my phone too. Charles or one of his friends must have picked it up and delivered it to him. Proof of a job done.

More likely, I'm just paranoid. Paranoid and very unlucky.

But none of that matters now. No, now I'm here for answers.

Once I pull the car into my usual spot between a few trees off the road, I awkwardly maneuver my limbs into the other clothes I brought, contorting myself between the panel of the door and the middle console. Such a relief to be out of that dress.

By the time I'm in my new clothes, the windows have fogged up. I lean forward over the steering wheel and use the sleeve of my coat to wipe a circle on the windshield. Nothing out there. Just trees. I hope. I exhale for what feels like the first time in twenty-four hours. Has it truly only been a day since I fell into the stream?

One breath. In. Out.

I leave my purse on the passenger seat and bury the car keys in my pocket, leaving the locked vehicle behind and finding the trail.

The dried pine needles crunch under my feet, forgotten and left for dead.

Stop it. Don't make this a bad place.

I let the crisp air fill my lungs. The quiet of the woods slows the racing of my heart. I can do this. Though I'm still unsure what happened yesterday, I can retrace my steps, see if it happens again. See if it connects with the dream or the strange card.

I hike until I hear the stream, stopping right before its edge to lower onto my hands and knees. Green moss tickles between my fingers, squishy and damp.

One breath. In. Out.

Slowly, I reach my hand down into the stream. The water is cold, and the current is slow. After a few minutes of waiting, my fingers turn numb. I sit back on my heels and rub my hand.

What am I missing?

Escape.

My bag is in the car, and I'm tempted to retrieve the card. But there's no need. The words are seared into my brain.

Escape.

Hazelgrove.

The solutions to the puzzle.

The solution to my problems? Is it insane to think that I didn't find that card by accident? If I allow myself to buy into the tiny whisper of hope in my heart, it feels more like fate.

But what does Hazelgrove mean? This town lacks anything bearing that name. Another code? My mind mulls over the possibility until it grows fuzzy.

I shove away from the stream and start pacing.

Whatever happened yesterday, it felt so real. More tangible than the same dream the night before. I was in a different forest from the one that surrounds me now. The tree cover was thicker, and the sky was darker. It smelled musty with decay, old wet leaves throwing off their scent from the ground. And the stream, it had grown. It wasn't slow and trickling. It was large, and the water rushed down it fast enough to soak my shoes in a matter of seconds. It was different.

I run my hands through my hair, my head pounding. My teeth pull on my bottom lip, biting down in frustration. Maybe my doctors were right, and I'm finally experiencing the psychotic break they predicted. Maybe I really can't tell the difference between imagination and reality. Isn't this exactly why my mother has been so insistent I take a different job? Because I'm too stressed out? She warned me there would be consequences, but I didn't want to listen.

My foot bumps against the fallen log, catching me off guard. I wind my leg back and kick the log hard. Which was stupid. Now I'm upset, and my foot hurts. Nice work, Sariah. I swallow the lump in my throat and steady my breathing.

One breath. In. Out.

I return to the trail and head towards the car, leaving the stream and the clearing behind.

EIGHT

How do I talk my way around things when I get home? It's been hours now, and I'd bet anything my mother has already called Copeland's office a dozen times to check on whether I came in. I drive towards Marshall's store, not sure where else to go. I pull into the parking lot, this day already too much like yesterday, and the déjà vu only serves to intensify my migraine.

Shaking, I drag my cracked cell phone from my bag and check the screen. Twelve missed calls and just as many text messages. All from her. I scroll through them. Each message grows more frantic.

I hurry to type with my good hand.

Emergency at the store. Took an extra shift. Couldn't make it to Erebus's office.

My fingers tap out his first name, trying not to gag. I need to appease her on some level. She always reminds me to address him as someone familiar.

I throw the phone back in the purse and sling the strap over my shoulder before exiting the vehicle. I need to move. Not ready to work yet, I bypass the front entrance and continue down the street. My toes graze the blue-painted pavement that designates the bus stop when a silver station wagon pulls up beside me, tires screeching, the passenger window rolled down.

"Sariah," a dark-haired man reaches over and opens the passenger door from the inside, peering out from the driver's seat, his seatbelt pulled taut as he ducks to look at my face. It's the man from yesterday. The stranger who got his face bashed in for me. "I know you don't know me, but this is important. I need to talk to you. Will you please get in?"

I turn and keep walking. No matter what he did, it doesn't change what happened last night. There's no way I'm getting into another car with a stranger. I don't even know his name.

A door slams behind me, and my stomach clenches as I sense him approach. Why didn't I bring something to defend myself? Haven't I learned my lesson by now?

"Sariah, please. Don't leave. I know this is crazy, and you have no reason to trust me, but please let me talk to you for one minute, and then you can decide to go. I won't stop you. I'll give you space, just hear me out." I turn and see that he's standing on the sidewalk beside his car. The passenger door hangs open. His hands raise so I can see his empty palms, his expression filled with distress.

"What do you want?" I keep my distance.

"You have dreams, right? Ones that seem real? Ones that come true?"

I stay silent. I don't discuss the dreams. Only with my doctors, and only selectively. How could someone I've never met possess that kind of information?

"I have them too," he goes on. "So do my brother and my

sister. We need your help."

"My help with what?" My instincts tell me to sprint to my car, but I've never met anyone else who has dreams like mine. Could he be lying?

An obnoxious string of bass notes increases in volume as a black SUV drives toward us. Its brakes release a high-pitched shriek as the driver comes into view and my whole body fills with lead, rooting my feet to the spot. Two attackers exit the vehicle, calling niceties at me, all too happy to run into me again. They stumble over their own feet, obviously intoxicated.

I can't move.

They're getting closer, and I know I should run, but my muscles lock in place.

Make it stop. Make it stop. Make it stop.

The blue-eyed man takes only a second to watch my lack of reaction before he comes over and wraps his arm around my shoulders, placing his body between them and me. A protective stance.

I don't feel any safer.

And I still can't move.

"Are these friends of yours, darling?" he calls out, standing tall. My gaze crawls up his chest to his face. He's staring the other two down. The scar on his forehead shines an angry red, though no longer bleeding. The men halt. I wonder if he landed a hit on either of them last night. "We were just leaving, sorry fellas." He ducks his head to whisper in my ear. "Are you ready to go?" His eyes find mine, and the desperation on his face pierces me. I falter, my eyes falling.

The swelling of his bottom lip has gone down since yesterday.

I force myself to meet those blue eyes. They bore into me.

"Okay," I choke.

He leads me to his car, his arm secured around me. His long fingers curl around my arm right below my shoulder. My steps are stiff and slow, but he doesn't rush me. Once I sink into the passenger seat, he closes the door with a light touch. The two men return to their SUV, one of them spitting in his direction, and then drive away as he sits down behind the steering wheel.

Will they leave? Or will they circle back around? Returning to my car alone poses a risk. My heart hammers in my chest.

"You don't have to come with me if you don't want to. You can get out of the car right now. But it seemed like those jerks scared you. Are you alright?" He focuses on me again.

My throat traps my voice. My breath comes out shallow. I struggle to move, apart from my shaking hands.

Not here. Please not here.

The sob rises from my chest as the tremors take over. I'm stuck to my seat, every part of me jittering. My eyes squeeze shut against the tears.

"Hey, oh, hey." The man grasps my hand with tenderness, then seems to think better of it, withdrawing. "It's okay. You can let it out. I won't hurt you. What can I do?" He glances around the car as if a solution could be hidden in the upholstery. "Let's breathe. I'll take some breaths, and you try to follow me, okay. In, two, three, four. Out, two, three, four. Slowly. In. Out."

I take a few minutes, but soon I latch on to the pattern,

putting all my focus on my breath, slowing it, calming it.

The shaking slows to a stop, my sore muscles relaxing. I look at him, feeling raw and confused.

"Who are you?" I whisper through an exhale.

He seems relieved to hear me speak, a smile hitching up one corner of his mouth. He has a strong jaw and a pale complexion. His eyes crinkle at the corners with his smile. "My name is Jace." Warm familiarity fills his gaze, but I'm sure we've never met before yesterday.

"And what exactly do you want?" He said he needed my help. Why would he need my help?

His smile falls.

"It's my sister," Jace starts. "She's missing. It's been a few days, and my brother and I can't find her. She's only thirteen." Panic underlines his words.

"That's terrible," I say. And I mean it. As a teenage girl in New Harper, she's already got a target on her back, and for her to be alone, to be missing... the possibilities aren't pretty. "But I don't know you. I don't know your sister. What makes you think I'll be able to help?"

He looks at his hands, chewing on his answer. "Because I've seen you. For a while. In my dreams. And when I saw you at the store, I couldn't believe it was you. It felt like a sign." He sighs. "I know how insane this sounds, and I want to explain. I want to answer your questions. Will you come with me? Back to my home? You can meet my brother, and we'll explain everything."

He must by lying. No one I've known has dreams like mine.

I've talked with enough psychologists to know it's not normal.

This is some sort of ploy. It always is with the men in this town. He's creative enough to make me come willingly. Crafting a narrative to pique my curiosity, to play on my fears.

That's what I want — to believe all the worst things about this man. Then I can leave and never look back.

But I see his fingers, the nail beds torn and picked at. The purple shadows under his eyes.

"Prove it." The words jump out of my mouth. I'm giving him a chance. Because I have to know.

"What?" His brows pull together.

"If you've had dreams about me, then prove it. Tell me something about myself. We've never met. If you know something about me that a stranger couldn't, then I'll know you aren't lying." Or that he's a liar who has somehow done his research, but maybe that's my paranoia cropping up.

"Okay." He pauses. He measures something in his mind as he looks at me again. "You love the forest. You prefer to wear black, never bright colors. You enjoy food but can often forget to eat." He doesn't take his eyes off me.

So far, he is correct, but I'm not convinced.

He continues. "You hate the commissioner. You don't feel safe in your home or in this town. You wish you could escape."

My heart falters.

He doesn't stop. "When you laugh, your left eye crinkles a little more than your right. And you snore when you sleep. Not in a bad way. Just a soft rumble."

Now he waits, still not looking away. His eyes trace the cheek that endured the worse scraping last night. "I left too soon, didn't I?" His voice carries pain now. It emanates from deep within his chest. I watch his knuckles turn white as he balls a fist.

Should I go with him? The questions flooding my mind will haunt me if I don't. I was ready to give up on myself. I thought I was crazy, but if he really has the dreams, maybe there's a chance he can help me too.

"I'll come," I say. "But I have to work my shift first."

"I'll wait," he jumps at the non-denial.

I turn away, trying to think straight. My leg bounces of its own accord. There are still a few hours until my shift, and I must look like a mess. I distract myself by pulling down the visor to check my reflection in the mirror.

A paperclip secures a photo there, blocking the glass. Three figures, their arms around each other, all of them mid-laugh. At first, it's the striking happiness radiating from them that gives me pause. I doubt I've ever looked like that. Then I see it. The girl in the photo, sandwiched between two tall men. One figure is Jace. The other must be his brother, who is just as tall though appears younger. Still a teenager, the closer I look.

I pull the photo from its perch, clasp it between my fingers.

"This is your sister?" I ask.

"Yes, that's Vanessa." He says her name, his voice filled with love and tinged with regret.

My eyes roam over her long dark hair. The voices from the forest echo back to me. That is what the other girl called her, wasn't it? She wears sneakers in the photo, with dirty shoelaces.

"I've seen her."

NINE

"WHEN?" JACE BREATHES. A light fills his face, a glimmer of hope.

How do I explain it?

Hazelgrove.

"It was yesterday morning." I begin. "Twice actually. Once in a dream, and once..." Was it another dream, or something else? How does a person fall into a different world? "Well, the second time it was like the dream again, but I wasn't sleeping. I felt like I was there."

"Where was she?" he presses.

"I'm not sure exactly. It was in a forest, but not our forest. I mean, I was in our forest, but then I wasn't. She wasn't." I sigh. I'm not making any sense. My head is pounding.

"Let me get you something to eat." Jace jumps in. "You're obviously dealing with a lot. You must be hungry."

My stomach gurgles on cue, and I curse it internally. I don't want to owe him any favors. I'm still deciding how I feel about this whole situation.

"No strings, just lunch. I swear." He puts a hand over his heart. Like I'm supposed to assume he's sincere. "When do you have to start work?"

I glance at the glowing lights of the dash and find the clock. 1:00pm.

My shift starts at five.

"One hour."

His lips pull down at the corners. "You're pretty early then." I nod. No need to elaborate. "Well, an hour is plenty of time. What do you feel like eating?"

I'm still not sure I should let him take me anywhere. But he's not wrong. I'm starving. "The deli nearby has good sandwiches."

"Great." He puts the car in gear.

"Let's walk." I burst out. Before he can protest, I grab the handle and burst onto the sidewalk. I shut it and lean in the window. "You'll need to get out of the bus area." I back up a few steps. It will be better if I'm not locked in the car. I'll talk to him, but I want the freedom to run.

He stares at me for a moment but turns forward and inches the car up the curb to an open spot. He rolls up the windows, then exits and locks the car, hurrying to meet me.

"It's this way." I walk briskly down the street, away from Marshall's shop. Faster than a normal pace, but he has no trouble keeping up. His legs are remarkably longer than mine. Which means running would not give me the advantage I hoped.

"So, you like the sandwiches here?" He asks casually. Like we could have a casual conversation. As if I could overlook for even a moment the fact that he also has dreams. That I'm not a single anomaly.

"Why haven't I seen you around?" I ask instead.

New Harper is not large. It's rare to encounter a new face.

He takes a breath, his eyes scanning our surroundings. "I don't exactly live in town."

I laugh. "What does that mean?"

There is nowhere else to live.

Jace drops his voice. "My family has a cabin out in the woods, on the edge of town. So not in town. We come in for supplies."

First Sophia, now a whole family hiding in the restricted outskirts of New Harper. Does the commissioner know?

Not that it matters. I'd never offer anyone up to Copeland. I'm not that cruel.

We reach the doors to the deli, and Jace pulls one open for me, the hot scent of fresh bread and melted cheese curling around me, dragging me forward into the crowded space. The emptiness of my stomach is a full-blown ache. The tip of my nose burns now that I'm out of the cold, and I feel Jace step in behind me, the door whooshing closed.

He bends his neck to speak in my ear, and I jump at the closeness.

"Sorry," he says, backing away an inch. "I was just going to ask, what's good? I've never been here before."

I take a moment to analyze his words, searching for the angle, for some way he could use the information against me. But it's an innocent question. "I like the number six. It has pepperoni, turkey, and provolone. The roast beef is good too."

Jace nods, searching the menu hanging above the counter. He lifts an arm to run his hand through his hair, the smell of pine drifting off him. The scent backs up his claim that he lives in the woods. I'm struck again by how tall he is. I'd never considered myself particularly short, but my nose only reaches his chest. The line moves forward, and we both take a step in unison.

I look at the floor. "So how does that work? Living outside of town."

He ducks his head again to whisper, and I try not to jump this time, focusing instead on a small stain that mars the collar of his worn brown jacket. "I shouldn't talk about it here, but I promise I'll tell you later. We can go there. I'll show you the cabin."

Promises from a stranger. Secrets and invitations. I shouldn't get myself mixed up in trouble. I've got my own problems. So why is my curiosity urging me to accept?

Questions sit ready on my tongue, but he's right. The place is packed with ears.

We shuffle the rest of the way to the silver counter in silence, and I settle into the feeling of his warmth behind me. When the cashier turns to take our order, Jace speaks first.

"We'll take a number six and a number eight." He fishes a card out of his pocket and reaches around me to hand it to the man at the register.

"Oh, you don't have to-" I start, but he cuts me off.

"Don't worry about it."

My cheeks flush as he takes the card back, and we sidestep to wait another moment while an employee wraps up our sandwiches in white and red checkered paper behind a short pane of glass. He marks the tape with a few letters and then passes the food to us.

"Thank you." Jace tells him.

My words are stuck in my throat. He doesn't think this is a date, does he? He motions for me to walk first and follows close behind. Holding both sandwiches in one hand at the door, he reaches over my head to push it open. I turn slightly to glance up at his face. When he notices, he smiles.

I quickly turn forward again and step out into the cold. Not good, not good, not good. I do not want to believe Jace is nice. That gives him too much power. I need to keep my head.

I move to sit on a cement bench around the corner, and Jace joins me.

"Number six for you?" He holds out the food.

I take it. The heat is welcome against my bare hands. Jace sets about unwrapping his sandwich. The roast beef. I watch him stuff a bite in his mouth, then lean back and swivel his head to scan the area while he chews. It's near deserted. Only an occasional passerby. The weather is less than appealing. The longer we sit, the more I can feel the cold bench biting under my legs. He doesn't rush to speak. Just takes another bite.

Might as well eat. My numbing fingertips pull at the tape, unfolding the paper to act as a makeshift plate in my lap. The waft of spices from the pepperoni makes my mouth salivate. I sink my teeth into the squishy bread and close my eyes, a groan escaping me.

My eyes fly back open, and I catch one corner of Jace's mouth hitch up for half a second. My cheeks blaze. I swallow the bite, then clear my throat. A man passes us on the sidewalk. When he's far enough away, Jace pauses his eating.

"I've lived in the cabin my whole life. My family has. My parents built it."

"Does the commissioner know?" I ask.

"If he does, he's never sent anyone to check on us. Not that I know of, anyway. We've been left alone out there."

I take a few more bites while he speaks.

"Like I said, we come into town to shop, stock up on supplies we can't get in the woods. But most of the time we try to keep to ourselves, not draw attention. My dad always told me it was safer that way. He didn't like Copeland. Said never to get involved with him."

I want to dig deeper into that. Into the subject of his parents, and their ability to build a home in the forest alone. How could they survive? What did they know about the commissioner? But there is another thought circling my brain, a more pressing one.

I force another bite down my dry throat. "When did you say your sister went missing?"

"Four days ago." His voice is hollow, the purple under his eyes growing deeper, like he hasn't slept a second since he realized she was gone.

"Did she mention anything out of the ordinary before she disappeared?" I know I saw her yesterday. But how? How would a girl from a secret cabin in New Harper end up running around in my dreams?

He thinks for a moment. "There was one thing. But I don't know what it means. The day before she vanished, she asked me about a word. I'd never heard it before, and I told her as much. That was it. She let the subject drop. But now I wonder where she learned the word."

"What word?" The hair on the nape of my neck rises in anticipation.

"She asked me if I knew the word 'hazelgrove'".

I crumple the checkered paper in my hand, jumping to my feet. I hitch my purse up on my shoulder and speed down the sidewalk, back towards the corner store.

"Sariah! Wait!" Jace calls after me.

I don't stop.

TEN

IN MY EXPERIENCE, COINCIDENCES are rare. And this feels coordinated, orchestrated even. The niggling thought rests at the base of my skull: I'm a player on a board. The question is, whose game am I playing?

I sense something amiss the second I walk into Marshall's shop. Conversations are hushed, and hardly anyone moves. Two male voices carry from the back. Marshall is in an argument with someone. Why do I get the sense it's about me?

I duck behind a shelf to listen but hear two people whispering in the next aisle.

"I remember when they delivered my boy. The kid might not be coherent right away. Their brains need time to adjust after the transfer before they function properly." A man's voice offers knowingly.

"That's good to know. I wasn't all that interested, to be honest, but my wife insisted she wanted one, so here we are." Says the other.

What are they talking about? I rush quietly to the aisle's end, and turn the corner, trying to view the individuals, but I bump into someone.

"Oh, I'm so sorry, I didn't see you." I stop to look at the woman I nearly knocked over. She teeters on a pair of stilettos but recovers.

"No harm done." She replies, straightening her blazer. She's dressed professionally and seems out of place here. But her face is vaguely familiar. I'd peg her to be early forties. Her brown hair is chopped neatly at her shoulders, accented by the clean lines of her jewelry.

"Can I help you find anything?" I realize I'm not in my uniform yet. "I work here. I just need to get ready for my shift. But I'm happy to help now."

"That's all right. I was waiting for my boss, but I imagine he'll be ready to leave any minute." She pulls out a sleek phone to check the screen.

"Do you work nearby?" Why am I still talking? I should just move on and leave her alone. But part of me wants to figure out where I've seen her before.

"Not especially nearby, no. I work at the city offices." She smiles. And before she can speak her next sentence, I place her. "I am the commissioner's personal assistant."

Over the shelf, I can see Commissioner Copeland emerge from the hall. If he's angry, he doesn't wear it on his face. All smiles for these citizens. He lifts a hand to slick the side of his hair back, then pulls a phone from his coat pocket.

"I have to go." The woman hoists a heavy leather tote bag onto one shoulder, rushing after him. He registers her with a glance, then continues through the exit. He doesn't hold the door, forcing her to catch it, balancing herself once again so she can heave it back open and follow.

I don't breathe until he's outside and out of sight through the windows. Everyone returns to normal once he's gone, the show over. Customers mill about the aisles, my coworkers herding items through checkout. As much as I want to run to the shelf, I make myself wait. Someone should check on Marshall.

His office door is open this time. The swivel chair faces the back wall, and a tall glass bottle hangs upside down in the air over it. I clear my throat. My boss turns, lowering the alcohol from his lips.

"Sorry, Sariah. I know I shouldn't drink on the clock." He screws the lid closed and stows the glass in the bottom right drawer of the desk.

I shrug. "You're in charge here."

"How much of that did you overhear?" He grimaces.

"Nothing, actually. What did he want?" My bag weighs heavy on my shoulder.

"The commissioner says I should impress upon you the importance of his offer. He made it clear that I will never be able to offer you the same benefits, and working here will never fulfill your needs." His fingers twitch as if he wants to reach for the drawer again.

"What did you tell him?" It should terrify me that Copeland tracked me down here, that he is so brazenly forcing his way into every part of my life.

But I can't help smirking at the agitation dripping off my boss. There's a sick comfort in the knowledge that not everyone has bought into the perfectly coiffed martyr-for-the-people act that our town's leader wears so well.

"That you're a grown woman and can make your own decisions." He huffs and stands.

"I'm sorry you had to deal with him."

"That's not your fault. I don't think he's ever liked me, but this shop consistently makes money, and even he's smart enough not to mess with something that's working." He waves me off. Then, he notices the clock. "You're early. I don't have you scheduled for a few more hours."

"Mind if I clock in? I can scrub something." Please don't turn me away.

Marshall sighs. "Why not? Get ready."

I oblige, darting to my locker.

Jace said he would wait for me until my shift ended, but that was before I abandoned him outside. I'm not sure he'll stick around now. But he did seem serious about his sister. I mull over leaving through the front entrance to find him, or instead using the rear door to get in my mother's car and drive away.

At my locker, I pull my phone out. No new messages from my mother, but I recall the one I sent to her a little while ago. Could that explain Copeland's appearance? She must have tipped him off. Regardless, I have the car, so hopefully she'll turn in for the night before I go home.

The sight of flowing black hair passes through my mind. Thirteen. So young. I can't understand what happened yesterday. But that was clearly Vanessa.

It's not something I've pondered before, but I don't know many people with siblings in New Harper. And Jace claims to have two. I wonder if it helps or hurts to have more people in your space. Personally, I've found that it's the people closest to you that hurt you the most. They're the ones you can't trust.

So, why do I want to trust Jace?

"Look alive, Invidia." Jodie brushes past me to jiggle open her own locker. For some reason, she likes to call me by my last name.

"Hey." I put my things into my locker, pull a polo over my long-sleeve shirt, and secure my name tag to it. We close our lockers in unison, leaving the room in a din of reverberating metal.

Jodie glances up at me as she fills out the sign-in sheet. "You doing okay? I heard about the fight in the alley. That guy you were helping was pretty cute." She smirks. Then focuses on my face, appalled. "What happened to you? Were you in the fight too?"

I drag my hair over my shoulder to block the worst of the wounds from sight. "I'm fine. Just tripped."

She gives me a dubious stare. "Right. Well, Marshall said you were patching up the guy after whatever happened back there. What'd you find out about him? We're stuck with the same dead-beat men constantly coming through here. This one was a welcome change of pace, don't you think?" She pumps her eyebrows, chewing on her thumbnail between her pink-glossed lips.

Jodie has always been one to gossip. I fiddle with the broken skin left from where I clawed open my hangnail. "Not much. He left pretty quickly." Maybe he is attractive, but that feeds my suspicion. Some people use any assets as tools to manipulate.

"Well, if he comes back around, send him my way." She winks and heads to her post.

I ignore her. We're not that good of friends. For all I know, Jace would be happy to meet her. I hardly know him anyway.

After signing in, I find a full cart in the hall. I commandeer it and start restocking shelves, trying to ignore how similar this is to last night. I don't need to think about Charles and his friends. I've done this task hundreds of times.

One breath. In. Out.

"Are those any good?" The voice startles me, though I know it now. Jace. "Sorry, I shouldn't have snuck up on you." He curses at himself under his breath. "I haven't tried that granola bar flavor. Is it new?"

I narrow my eyes at him. "We just got the shipment in from the factory yesterday, so I guess." It is the first time I've seen this flavor. The shiny label reads: Maple Fusion. Whatever that means. "Would you like one?" I extend the bar to him, hoping to keep him at arm's length.

"No, thank you." He takes two steps towards me and reaches over my shoulder. When he speaks, his mouth is inches from my ear. "I prefer the chocolate." He withdraws, a wrapper crinkling in his hand.

I realize I've stopped breathing.

"What about you? Do you have a favorite?" He holds the granola bar at his side and stuffs his other hand in the pocket of his blue jeans. I make my arms move again, lining up more of the bars in orderly rows. Should I keep talking to him?

He knows about the dreams. And has his own. Although my instinct is to ice him out, he has information, both about me and that I want. I'll have to play the game.

"I like to keep maple on my donuts. As for granola bars, I'll have to agree with you." I nod at the chocolate-flavored bar in his hand.

The corner of his mouth hitches up. Jodie enters the aisle and walks behind me to grab one of the boxes from the cart. When she makes it past Jace, she turns and shoots me a thumbs up. I study my shoes.

"Is there anything else I can help you find?" I keep my tone professional.

"I think I've got it from here." He steps towards me again, this time brushing past me and lowering his voice. "I'll meet you outside when you're ready." He swipes a second bar and heads down the aisle. My eyes track him as he zigzags through the store and grabs a few other items. He glances up at me a few times while waiting at checkout. I try my best to keep busy, not to let him distract me.

His eyes catch mine when he heads out the door. He smiles. A full smile, just for a second before it drops, and he leaves.

Maybe I won't ditch him.

First, I have to check something.

I leave the cart and wind around to the feminine products. A strange sensation creeps up my neck, and I remember the way the dense trees enclosed me in shadows, the sudden pull in my gut as I fell into the stream. My hand trembles, inching towards the first box of pads. I need to search the shelf for any other paper scraps, any other codes. The green one I found is still in my purse, stuffed in my own box of pads.

One breath. In. Out.

I pull the box from the shelf, and the metal is bare.

From the corner of my eye, I spot something green flutter to the ground.

My breath hitches. I stoop down to peel the rectangular paper from the tile. The same holes. The same string of numbers.

Someone hid a new paper here since last night.

Someone, or something, knew that it needed replacing. Does that mean whoever it is knows that I took it?

I hate the feeling of being watched. I whirl my head back, checking for prying eyes. But I'm alone.

ELEVEN

My footsteps falter exiting the store hours later. The street sits deserted, not a car in sight. He left?

Who am I kidding? Of course he left.

I huff a mirthless laugh at myself and turn to wrap around the brick building to the parking lot. My reflection catches in the dark glass, and I jump. The bruises have started changing color, and I forgot to put on makeup today. Splotches of purple and green climb the pale skin of my neck and the right corner of my mouth. No wonder everyone keeps asking if I'm okay.

While the commissioner would deny condoning assault, there aren't any fixed rules about it in this town. Calling the guard could provide me with a medic, but the consequences for aggressors would be minimal. Everyone knows it. That's why I like working for Marshall. He's intimidating enough to scare off the jerks. Most of the time.

I tear my eyes from my reflection and move my feet. It's dark out, and I shouldn't loiter here where anyone could be waiting in the shadows. I turn the corner as Jodie pulls out of the parking lot, her taillights illuminating three other cars, bathing them in red. One is Marshall's. My mother's sits next to it. And a silver station wagon.

The latter roars to life, blinking yellow beams at me.

One breath. In. Out.

Approaching slowly, I bend to look in the passenger window. Jace opens his own door and stands, smiling at me over the top of the car. He rounds to my side and opens the door, the hinge's creak splitting the night air. I swivel and retreat until my back hits the hard wall of the building.

Jace's smile falls. "You don't have to come. Not if you don't want to. I'll admit I got my hopes up." He casts his eyes to the ground and laughs at himself, scratching behind his ear. "But it's up to you. I can understand if you don't want to come with me." He sounds so genuine.

I weigh my options. Go home with no answers and continue living each day in fear. Or take a chance on the man in front of me.

I can do this. I just have to keep my guard up.

One breath. In. Out.

I step forward and slide into the passenger seat. He regards me, his expression unreadable. Then he closes the door gently and joins me in the car.

"I thought you might be hungry. Sorry, is it weird that I keep asking you about food? I just know that I get hungry, and that was such a long shift." He trails off and reaches for a rectangular box resting on the dash, then offers it to me.

I accept it to avoid being awkward and immediately recognize the stamp. I glance at him, then open the box to peek inside. Two glistening maple bars.

Okay, maybe I can let my guard down a little.

Even if this is a bribe of some sort, I need him to think I trust him, so he'll open up when I ask him my questions.

He clears his throat. "Feel free to dig in. You sure you're ready to go?"

I look over at my mother's car. I could take the out.

"I'm sure. Let's go."

Jace shifts gears. "It's a bit of a drive."

WE'VE BEEN DRIVING FOR an hour when he slows on the main road and makes a sharp turn into a gap between the trees. I can barely make out the semblance of a dirt path as we bump over rocks and tree roots. This is much farther than my hiking spot.

"Almost there, I promise." He scans the forest and pulls between another pair of trees. Everything goes dark.

I can't help it when my heart speeds. Did I let a murderer drive me into the remote woods outside of town? Why didn't I grab something to use as a weapon?

A flashlight clicks, illuminating our feet but providing enough light that I can see Jace's face. "We walk from here. When you get out, walk straight back. That'll lead you out of the garage. I'll lock things up."

I follow his directions, my heart in my throat as I traverse the dark den. The scraping sound of my shoes in the dirt mirrors Jace's footsteps on the opposite side of the car.

I break past the tall pines, and moonlight reveals what he meant by garage. Long-needled branches disguise the constructed cavern. He lowers a rolling door, the slats whispering on wheels, then arranges branches to appear like any other copse of trees.

When he emerges from the greenery, he looks me over and fails to keep the corner of his mouth down. He clears his throat. "Follow me. It's not too far, but it's easy to get turned around out here."

He leads me back and forth through the trees. We don't seem to be taking any particular direction, then I see it. A small cabin, big enough for two modest rooms. The windows are dark. The quiet of the forest presses in on me. No car engines, no doors slamming, no voices. Only the soft thud of Jace's boots on the three stairs attached to the porch. I climb a step behind him. Jace slides a key into the door and holds it open.

One breath. In. Out.

Getting into the car with him was one thing. A confined space deep in the woods where no one is around to hear me scream? That unsettles me.

"It's better on the inside." He's watching me. From this close, I can smell him, more than just the pine needle aroma. I smell laundry powder and freshly chopped wood and a natural musk underneath that must belong to him. Is he as nervous as I am? Or was this his plan all along? To isolate me, to make me offer myself willingly. He could pin me in his arms in a second if he wanted to. I present no physical challenge. If this is a trap, I've miscalculated mentally as well. My only option is to go along with what he says.

I must avoid provoking him.

I inch my foot over the threshold, pressing my back against the wall beside the door. The least I can do is make sure I see him coming.

A black wood stove with a chimney stands in the center of the room. The kitchenette to the left includes a door, a pantry I assume, due to its modest width. A few chairs take up the other corner, with a circular table between them. Dust coats the tabletop in a thick, unmarred layer. For a place supposedly occupied for decades, the room looks eerily untouched.

Jace enters and locks the door behind him. My heart stops with the thud of the deadbolt.

"The door is over here." He walks to the pantry and opens it. All I see is an empty little closet, but he steps inside and looks to me, waiting.

"Is there a reason you're standing in a pantry?" I narrow my eyes at him.

"It's the entrance. To our house. Get in, I'll show you." He shuffles to the back wall, though there's hardly enough space for him alone. "I could send you down first, but it will be faster if we go together."

Down?

I eye the floorboards, wondering what sort of pit must exist below. Jace watches me while I stand debating.

It's possible I have a death wish, because I cross the stale room and step into the closet. Less than an inch separates Jace and me, and that inch disappears when he stretches his arm around me to close the door. Once again, I'm in the dark. My spine is rigid as Jace's soft breath falls against the top of my head. The warmth of it makes me realize how cold my toes have gotten.

Don't panic.

One breath. In. Out.

"One second," he whispers, and I hear him move something near the top of the wall. With one click, a dim light shines down over us. Another click and a grinding begins. The floor drops from under me, and I have to brace my core to keep from stumbling into Jace. We're moving down.

Moving my eyes upward, I catch Jace's gaze settled on my face, faraway, almost like he's looking through me. Our proximity is loud in my ears. I press against the wall behind me as much as I can, then with a whoosh it disappears, and I reel backward. Before I can hit the floor, Jace's arms are around me, pulling me into him, securing my feet to the ground. My body burns at his touch, bruises on my back painfully tender, and all I see are the four men last night, all the fear flooding back into my limbs.

"Are you alright?" The panic in his voice makes it seem like I almost died, rather than landed on my rear end. I snap out of it.

"I'm fine." I extricate myself from his hold, stepping back to put a few paces between us.

"Sorry," he blurts. "I'm sorry." He scrunches his eyes closed, pinching them with a finger and thumb, and shakes his head. "Let's find my brother."

Once I turn around, I'm surprised to see what looks like a much larger home. A kitchen and dining table are on my left.

An arch in the back wall leads to a hallway lined with more doors. Couches and an old television fill the living room before us.

"No search necessary," a voice says. Another dark-haired individual rises from where he was lounging on one of the couches. The teenager in the photo. He takes the two of us in with his arms crossed over his chest. "You really found her?" he says to his brother, disbelieving. Jace nods. "Well, welcome." He stretches one hand out to me, and I shake it tentatively. "I'm Ian. Come, sit down."

His voice isn't as deep as Jace's, his frame a bit lankier, but the similarities between the two are undeniable. I pick a spot on the opposite couch, studying both men. They share dark hair, blue eyes, and tall builds.

"What have you told her?" Ian asks his brother, settling back into his seat.

"That V is gone. And we need her help." Jace takes the spot beside his brother. Facing each other, we all take a collective breath.

Curiosity burns my tongue, sending the question flying from my mouth. "You both have dreams?"

The brothers share a glance.

"Yes," Ian replies. "All three of us. Jace, our sister, and I have had the dreams since we were young. Our mom did too. It's a little different for each of us. But the dreams are real—they come true."

"Your mom. Where is she now?" I can't overlook the sinister word did.

"There was an accident. Our parents were searching for answers, trying to understand why we were all having these dreams. One day they tried looking somewhere new, but they never came home." Ian focuses on our conversation, sitting on the edge of his seat, firing off answers. But Jace looks down, eyes glazed.

"Somewhere new? Like a different part of the woods? Or do you mean a new doctor? I've talked with every psychologist in town. None of them has ever had an explanation for the dreams besides delusion." My mother included, though I don't mention that aloud.

"No. They went somewhere outside of New Harper." Ian answers.

My eyebrows draw together. "There is nowhere outside of New Harper."

Ian looks at his brother. "We need to show her."

Jace shakes his head. "We don't need to overwhelm her. We can do this slowly."

"Vanessa has already been gone for days. We don't have time to take it slow."

Sweat forms on my lower back. I scan my surroundings for anything I can grab to defend myself if these men turn on me. A pen sits abandoned on the coffee table between us. I lean forward and pick it up, spinning it between my fingers, pretending I only plan to fidget with it. It's not much, but the pointed end is better than nothing.

"I need to understand what I'm doing here." I voice. "Otherwise, there really isn't any point in my staying." It's a bluff. Based on the seclusion of their home, I'd guess Copeland has no idea they are out here. Which, if they let me stay for a while, makes this a perfect hideout. But I can't get ahead of myself. I need to learn their intentions. I may be desperate, but I can't let myself be stupid.

Jace looks stricken. He heaves a breath through his nose. "Okay."

Ian takes the word as his cue, jumping from the couch and striding across the room to a paneled wall.

Jace also rises and offers me a hand. I ignore it, standing on my own. The outstretched hand goes to rub the back of his neck. "You can follow Ian. We'll show you the lab."

I keep the pen gripped in one fist and motion for Jace to walk first, not wanting anyone behind me. Ian has opened a small square of the paneling and is punching buttons with his finger. A shrill beep precedes a whir of gears.

A piece of the wall recedes into itself and pulls to one side, leaving a black door-sized hole. Both men walk through, and white lights click on, bouncing off every metal surface and glass screen. The term lab certainly fits. Enough computers to rival the city offices sit on long tabletops. Cases with glass windows hold vials and tubes and ominous medical instruments. They make the pen in my hand feel frivolous. The farther we walk, the less familiar the contraptions become, messes of wires and metal components.

"There's something you should see." Ian rolls out a chair to sit before one of the many screens. His fingers fly over a keyboard, and a news report fills the screen. I've seen the New Harper news broadcast. My mother watches it every morning. But the banner across the bottom of the screen doesn't say New Harper. The letters are strange-looking, and the reporter is speaking gibberish. Ian clicks a key. Another newscast, this one different. He continues through three more until landing on New Harper's broadcast.

The only one I'm familiar with.

"What was that?" New Harper has exactly two television channels. One is a 24-hour news broadcast. The other is an entertainment channel. They film at the local studio downtown.

Ian turns back to me. "You said there is nowhere outside of New Harper. That's not actually true. The government here works extremely hard to make everyone believe that. Copeland wants you to think this is the only place in existence. To feel stuck within the confines of this town. In reality, we're one small pocket in a much bigger world full of municipalities."

Ache blooms at the base of my skull. That's not right. There's New Harper and the woods surrounding it. That is all there has ever been. The more I dwell on the thought, the fuzzier its edges seem.

"Where do you get your water?" Ian asks me.

What a strange question. "I use tap water. Everyone uses tap water." I rub my neck, trying to dampen the discomfort. Where is he going with this?

"They're lying to you. Everyone in New Harper has been placed in a bubble. The government controls everything we have access to: the water, food, medicine, information — it's all fed to us at the discretion of the commissioner." My spine stiffens at his last word. I know all too well that the town's beloved leader has a dark side. But this is absurd.

Ian continues, his voice urgent, each sentence pouring out of him. "Let me ask you a few questions, and you think about them for a minute, okay? Why is it called 'New' Harper? If it's the only place that's ever been on Earth, what makes it new? Where do we all come from? Have you ever seen a child under the age of ten? Do you remember anything before you were ten?"

I mull over the questions, struggling to process them. I've done my best to block out most of my childhood years. I push back in my mind, trying to remember. The harder I try, the more pronounced the pain in my head becomes. I can't think past the earliest memories of when I was ten, so many of them filled with Commissioner Copeland. My hands start to shake. I struggle to regain composure.

One breath. In. Out.

But my breaths are coming too fast. I can't slow them down. I press a hand to my head, trying to stop the pulsing pressure building inside my skull.

"That's enough, Ian. Let's give her a break." Jace moves to put a hand on my other arm, but I snatch it away, hugging it into my chest. "Sariah, I'm sorry. This is a lot to take in. We've always known. The three of us were born in this cabin. Our parents raised us apart from New Harper. They recognized something was wrong a long time ago. But you asked why we want you here." Jace speaks softly, searching my face. "My brother and I haven't been able to see our sister, Vanessa, in any of our dreams. Usually we're connected, the three of us. We have a sense of each other. But ever since she disappeared, it's like she's cut off. Who I do see in my dreams is you. I think you can help. I think you can find her."

He looks so hopeful. He really believes I'm his best option. I don't even know him, but it hurts my heart to see how much he cares. That hurt breaks through the panic enough for me to speak.

"I've never been able to control the dreams," I murmur. "It doesn't work like that. They just happen." I look away. Why do I wish so much that I could help them? I don't even know if I can trust anything they're saying. A picture frame sitting on the desk catches my eye. I lean to the side to see it better over Ian's shoulder.

The photo is captivating, but I don't understand what I'm looking at.

"What is that?" I nod toward the picture.

Both men turn to look.

"That's Vanessa," Jace answers. "When she was a baby."

"Baby?" I roll the foreign word over in my mouth. The shining blue eyes do match the ones that whipped toward me in the dream forest. But in this photo, flawless, squishy skin surrounds them. Her head must be tiny. It's not like anything I've ever seen before.

Why is my brain on fire? The pen clatters to the ground as I press both palms into my eyes, gripping my scalp with my fingertips, trying, and failing, to push the pain away.

"It's too much for her. I told you we need to go slower." Jace grumbles. I feel his hands on my shoulders, but I wrench myself away from the touch.

One breath. In. Out.

I regain my composure and face Jace and Ian. My face is hot, eyes stinging with the threat of tears. I want to claw out whatever is stuck in the back of my skull. But I resist. I push against the pain and settle my face into a neutral expression.

Don't feel it.

Push it down.

I've had plenty of practice pretending I'm okay.

I rub my sweaty palms down the sides of my pants.

"I'll help you." I start. "But you'll need to help me too."

TWELVE

MOVES AND COUNTERMOVES.

Piecing the puzzle together bit by bit. I can make this work. I have information they need, and they can buy me a few days away from Copeland. It would be a greater escape than I've ever dared to hope for.

My mind flits to the green card in my bag. I'll show them. Eventually. So far, their answers have only produced more questions. I should gather all the information I can while they are so forthcoming.

The water cup trembles in my hand, though not as violently as before. I take a sip, the brown cushions of the couch attempting to swallow me whole.

"I'm sorry." Jace repeats. "I know this must be a lot to take in."

"I'm okay." I assure him.

If I'm honest, it's not what they're telling me that has me on edge. It's what happened yesterday morning. The dreams have been a constant throughout my entire life. But falling into that stream was not just another nightmare. I went somewhere. I left New Harper. A thrilling notion. But also terrifying.

I know the monsters in this town. I have no way of knowing what might lurk beyond its borders.

"Could I fix that up for you?" Jace is looking at my hand. The bandage from earlier hangs loose and pathetic around my palm. It's a surprise it made it through my shift at all. Now that he mentions it, the cut does sting.

I consider declining, but what good would that do me? "That would be very helpful, thank you." I set down the cup and dab my mouth with the back of my good hand.

He comes back with a first-aid kit, this one much more extensive than the plastic white box in Marshall's office. He rolls it out on the coffee table, revealing neat pockets and rows of bandages, wipes, scissors, clamps, pills. Enough supplies for a medical office. Makes sense if they have really been secluded in the woods all this time.

"I'm glad I get to return the favor." Jace says as he sinks into the cushion next to me. "Not that I'm glad you're hurt, I just mean—" He groans, hiding his face in his palms.

I'm tempted to laugh, but I don't know if he's hiding a temper. I don't want to risk setting him off. The smallest smile takes over my lips. When he looks back up at me, he sighs.

"I'm sorry. It shouldn't be this hard to talk to you. I guess I don't want to ruin my first impression." He removes the bandage from my palm and lifts my hand in both of his to inspect the cut. "Though, come to think of it, I guess I already did that by getting punched in the face." He glances up at me through his eyelashes, the beginning of a smirk tugging at his mouth again.

"It looks a lot better." I say. "Your face. It's not swollen anymore." The wound on his temple has scabbed over cleanly. No thanks to me, I'm sure, based on how skillfully he cleans and bandages my hand. His fingers are deft and precise in their movements.

He eyes my neck and mouth, not yet letting go of me. "Looks like I left too soon." I swear his eyes go dark, the clear blue of sunshine on still water churning into the rain that falls from storm clouds. "I didn't think they'd come back. If I'd known, I wouldn't have left your side. I'm so sorry, Sariah." His sincerity hits me in the chest.

"There's no way you could have known." I lean back, pulling my collar up with both hands, and sweeping my hair forward to hide the rest of the bruises. "Besides, you don't owe me anything. It's not your job to keep me safe. We barely know each other."

He opens his mouth but closes it again. Instead of speaking, he tidies the supplies.

"What time is it?" I ask.

He checks his watch. "Three in the morning. I'm happy to set up a room for you with a bed. You can get some sleep."

Is he already assuming I'll stay? I need to think this through. How much do I say?

"I have to take my mother's car back to our house. She'll need it to go to work, and if it's not there she'll worry, call a search party." She'll need to leave in three hours, and it will take half that time to drive back into town and get the car home. I have to convince him to drive me back quickly. I don't want to give Copeland any more incentive to find me.

"Of course." He nods, a bob in his throat as he swallows. "Will you…" He trails off, looks at the ground.

"What?" I press. I need to know what he's thinking.

He turns to me. "Will you want to come back? Or have you decided you'd rather go home?" His spark of hope wavers toward extinguishment. That shouldn't bother me. I shouldn't be invested in his feelings. But the thought of disappointing him tugs at my stomach. Or maybe that's the menstrual cramps.

"I would like to come back. If that's okay? It's just that she can't know I'm leaving. I'll have to sneak out. And I'll have to ditch my phone." A part of me has always suspected it's bugged somehow. Especially since the commissioner brought it back after the other night. It may be paranoia, but why take the chance?

"What's wrong with it?" His relief is palpable. Already, he's shifted gears to problem-solving.

"Nothing. I just don't trust it."

"May I?" He holds out a hand. I reach into my pocket and dig the phone out. I hesitate for only a fraction of a second before giving it to him.

Immediately, he jumps up and heads back toward the lab hidden behind the wall. I could stay here. Let the couch eat me. Maybe there's another hidden room inside.

I stand, making sure I have my footing before following. He's already got the phone plugged in to a workstation when I catch up. The screen rolls out a string of numbers I don't understand.

Jace spits a curse at the computer.

The outburst startles me. "What is it?"

"There's a code here that signifies the commissioner's office. It means a computer in that building has access to all the information on your phone. It's been hacked, to put it simply." He glares at the screen, then turns to me. "How could you tell?"

"Just a feeling." I don't mention that this is one of Copeland's tamer crimes.

"Would you like to smash it?" He unplugs it and holds it out to me. I take it.

"Wouldn't they see if it suddenly went dead?" While I'd love to be rid of the tie, it's a piece on the board. I don't want to sacrifice it without thinking it through.

Jace bites his lip. "Yeah, probably."

"I'll save it for now." I slip it into my back pocket, my next move taking shape in my head.

"Well, if we're going to be sneaking around, I need a way to contact you. And there is no way I'm putting my number into that thing." He walks to a cabinet and digs around.

When he turns, he brandishes another black phone. A model or two behind mine, but in considerably better shape. "Let me just put my number in. And Ian's. I'll send myself a message so I can save your number." He pulls out his own dated phone to check that it works.

"Now, I will be upfront with you that we attached GPS to this. I don't think we have time to disable it, but I want you aware, in case that's a problem."

I curl my fingers around the plastic. "Thank you."

OUTSIDE THE WOODS ARE pitch dark. I rely on the beam of Jace's flashlight to get back to the station wagon. The hum of the road under its wheels threatens to lull me to sleep, so I start the conversation.

"You'll probably think this is a stupid question..." Do I even want to ask?

"I'm sure it's not." He peeks at me before facing the road again.

I take a breath. "What is a baby?"

His jaw clicks. He weighs his answer before speaking. "It's how a person enters the world. Small, and then they grow bigger. Prior to age ten, you were nine, then eight, et cetera. When a person is zero, that's called a baby."

I don't understand. Pain floods my skull in a surge. Logically, it makes sense that I was younger than ten at some point. I must have existed before then. "Why can't I remember it?"

"It's part of how the commissioner keeps control. We told you. He drugs the water. Part of that cocktail is a memory inhibitor. My parents told me that no one started out their lives in New Harper. Well, except for us kids. We were born here, like I said. But they told me that everyone else had been brought here. Assigned here." He looks at me again to see how the words are hitting me.

"So, what? Copeland just picked a bunch of families and transplanted them into his town somehow?" It sounds like total nonsense.

"Not so much families as individuals. Remember how you've never seen young kids around?" He lets that linger in the air.

"Sure. But I live with my mother. I haven't been alone my whole life." Even if it feels like I have.

"Sariah." Jace pauses. The trees fly by the windows, looming shadows on either side of us. He swells and finally speaks. "The reason my parents went into hiding, the reason they built our home outside of town, is because Copeland wanted to start recruiting children for the population. Not families. Children. Hand picked. His plan was to bring them in and assign them a guardian. Someone to pretend to be their parent. To create a sense of normality."

I know Erebus Copeland is a sadistic, selfish snake. But what Jace is proposing is on a whole other level of megalomania. And why is my head on fire?

"What are you saying?" I demand.

Jace sighs. "I'm saying the woman you've lived with since you were ten years old is not your mother."

THIRTEEN

I NEVER GUESSED IT would hurt so much when my sorry excuse for a life shattered into hundreds of jagged pieces. Everything was a lie. All of it. My chest burns, the impact of the words striking me like a knife. But the heat churns into something beyond hurt. My finger throbs again as my pulse quickens. The worst part might be that I can't decide if this revelation makes me hate my mother — hate Audrey — more or less. It must have been easier to serve me up for Copeland's whims if she didn't have a real reason to care about me.

It's no wonder she insisted I live with her, even progressing into my adult years. She put all her reasons into my head. Why I need her. Why I would never be able to cope on my own. But that wasn't it at all. She was the guard tasked with holding me captive.

Not anymore.

When we pull up next to her car in the parking lot, I slam the door of the station wagon behind me, not caring who may hear. Any of the panic that usually lives inside me is snuffed out by rage. I can feel the blood pooling in my limbs, my stomach twisting. I want to drive my fist through the brick wall. Better yet, I could drive her car through it.

When a pair of hands grip my shoulders, I spin around, swinging my arm so that my punch can find a target. Jace doubles over with a wheeze. I got him right in the stomach. It's enough to snap me out of my rampage. What am I doing? I don't hurt people.

"Jace, I'm so sorry. I didn't mean to." I reach for him, to hold him steady.

"That's alright." He grunts. "I probably deserved it. My explanation could have used more tact." He straightens and sucks in air through rounded lips, pushing his dark hair back from his forehead. His eyes fall to my face, and that smirk returns. "At least tell me it felt good."

Is he joking? "No, I feel horrible!"

"Of course! Of course. But I mean the punch. It felt good to take a whack at something, right?" He massages his abdomen where I made contact.

There's a buzz in my ears, the adrenaline fading. "Maybe a little." I admit.

He laughs. "Better me than your ride, I suppose. I'd like to get you home in one piece. Got any more you need to unload? I can brace myself this time." He widens his stance, tensing his muscles and squinting. He looks ridiculous.

It's my turn to laugh. The sound flutters from my chest. When was the last time I laughed? The thought sobers me, bringing tears to my eyes. Stupid. Don't cry now. You're running out of time as it is.

"Let's go. You can follow me, just pull past the house down the street a ways and I'll meet you as soon as I can."

I'm really doing this. I'm going to run away with this stranger.

I have to backtrack to his car to grab my bag, and then I pull the keys from my coat to unlock Audrey's.

One breath. In. Out.

I can do this. I start the engine and shift into reverse, backing out of the spot. No going back now. I finally have a chance to choose for myself. As I pull out of the parking lot, I check my rearview mirror to make sure Jace is following me.

The streets are empty at this hour, making the drive home quick. I ease the car onto the driveway as quietly as I can manage, though everything feels amplified in the silence of night. Outside, I round the corner to use the service entrance. I don't want to risk the rumble of the garage door waking Audrey. I grip the keys carefully when inserting them in the door, holding onto all the loose ones so they don't jangle against each other.

Crossing the dark space to the entrance, I'm filled with gratitude that my room is closest to the garage. With any luck, Audrey won't hear me from her bedroom on the other side of the house. I take my sneakers off before crossing the threshold, padding over the floorboards in my socks. I hold my breath until I enter my bedroom. My hands start to shake as I grasp the door handle, holding it down so the latch won't make a sound when I press it closed.

Exhale.

My bed invites me to lay down, my blankets still twirled up in a nest like I left them. But this isn't my home anymore.

It can't be.

I set to work pulling my largest bag from my closet and stuffing in clothes and belongings I don't want to leave behind. It's not much, but it will have to be enough for a new start. I've got my savings. My own apartment may be out of the question now, but that means I can use the money to buy whatever else I need. This will work.

A creak echos from down the hall.

She's awake.

I toss the bag onto the floor of my closet and strip off my coat to throw on top. Then I lunge for the bed as stealthily as I can manage. Not graceful, but quiet enough. Hopefully.

I lay down and watch the door. The knob turns slowly.

She is trying to be quiet too.

The gap widens, shadows on the floor crisscrossing, pushing at each other. Her silhouette fills the doorway. I close my eyes. She waits silently.

After a moment, she steps forward, coming to hover over my bed. I feel her warm hand on my arm, rousing me from sleep with the same gentleness she's always used. I feign grogginess, blinking and sitting up to switch on the lamp.

Her lips purse in concern. "When did you get home?"

I rub my eyes to play for time. I can't count on the assumption that she's been asleep. For all I know, she's been awake waiting for me to get back. Vague is better.

"Not too long ago. It was a late night." I really should have figured out my story before I came inside.

"I can't believe your boss had you work back-to-back shifts.

It's just not healthy. Making you work all day and all night. And to keep you so much later than usual. It's nearly morning! I'm going to report him."

"No!" I burst out. "I mean, no, he didn't keep me late." I won't let Marshall take the fall for this.

"So, where precisely have you been this entire evening?" Her eyebrows approach her hairline.

I have to lie.

"I was with C—with Erebus." She prefers me to use his first name. Tells me he's a family friend, not just some politician. That I should be comfortable being familiar with him.

"Oh?" Her eyes light up at just the mention of him. "I thought you weren't able to see him yesterday." She's ready to call my bluff.

"I wasn't. But after I finished at work, I called him. You said it was important for me to schedule a meeting with him. He was still awake, so he let me come and talk with him." Will she buy it?

"So, you've been with Erebus this whole time?" She says his name with a reverence that churns my insides.

I read between the lines of the question.

It's clear now that I was wrong. I gave her too much credit all these years. Assuming she was blind to the situation. Believing she couldn't know what the object of her adoration was doing to her own daughter.

It's written on her face in the honeyed light that bleeds through the lampshade.

She's always known.

"Yes. I was with him all night."

Her reaction is a mixture of satisfaction and disappointment. I need to make her leave. And I know just what she wants to hear.

"He told me he wished he could see you. That he's been thinking about you."

Her cheeks turn pink. "He did? Well, perhaps I'll go see him today." The wheels are turning in her head, scheming a way to show up at his office casually, I'm sure.

"He would like that." I want to vomit.

She pats my arm absently. "You get some sleep, sweetheart. You must be exhausted." She bends to place a kiss on my temple before clicking off the lamp.

When the door latches shut behind her, I allow only two tears to fall down my cheek. I use my sleeve to wipe them away.

One breath. In. Out.

FOURTEEN

I STAY IN MY bed until I hear Audrey's shower splash on. I would kill for a shower. But this is my shot.

I pull the two phones from my back pocket and flip the lamp switch. I leave the dented phone powered on and set it atop the table. Should I make it harder to find? I need it to ping back to this room if it's being tracked. Who knows how exact the location tracking is? At a minimum, I need it to show up inside the house. That way it looks like I'm here. As far as anyone else will know, I'm sleeping in my room for the next eight hours.

What will it look like after that? If I leave it on the table, Audrey will assume I forgot it when I went to work. Will she try to bring it to me? Probably not. She won't worry until I'm not home tomorrow morning.

If I hide it in a drawer or a closet, she might not notice it. She'll assume I have it with me. If she tries to contact me, it will seem like I am deliberately not answering. But that might make her more frustrated. She could call Copeland and ask him to check up on me. Again. Any excuse to talk to that man.

Table it is. I turn the sound off, so it won't make any noise while I'm gone. Then, I turn my attention to the new phone.

The screen illuminates, and I realize this one must be silenced as well. A string of messages, all from Jace.

> Did you make it in?

> Are you okay?

> Do you need help?

> Please answer me.

> Sorry, I'll try to be patient. I'm parked not too far away.

> Okay, it's been almost an hour. I'm worried. Where are you?

I take pity on the man and type a reply:

> Leaving house now.

I yank my coat back on and secure the strap of my bag over my shoulder. With my house keys in one hand and my new phone in the other, I press an ear against the door. The stream of water falls in interrupted bursts. She must be in there now. This is it. I move swiftly, securing the bedroom door behind me, then locking the service door to the garage with a solid click.

Outside, the sky has filled with gray, night dying out, the sun threatening to break the horizon. I walk just in case anyone else is out. My feet itch to move faster, to run, but I won't risk being noticed in this moment. I need to vanish like ice melting into water.

I was here until I wasn't, and no one can pinpoint my disappearance.

The phone screen lights again.

I see you.

Up ahead, an engine growls. It's Jace. If I make it to that car, I have a chance at a clean slate. A new life. My back prickles. Is someone watching me, or am I getting in my own head?

Don't look back. Don't cause suspicion. Just keep moving. I clear the back bumper. Two more steps and my hand wraps around the door handle. When I pull, I let myself cast a sweeping look behind me. No one. But my back still tingles.

It doesn't matter. I throw my bag to the floor and climb in, gripping the door even after it's closed. Jace wastes no time pulling forward. He starts slowly, but after we make a few turns and see no one else around, he presses on the gas pedal.

"Were you seen?" He finally asks.

"Audrey talked to me when I first came inside. But she shouldn't suspect anything." Not right away, at least. The nagging sensation of being watched is fading. It must be my brain playing tricks on me.

Jace keeps checking the mirrors. His under-eyes are darker now, purple in the crease of his eye socket nearest his nose. I wonder when he last slept.

"How are you?" He croaks. It could pass as a normal question any other time, but with everything that has happened, everything I've learned, and the choice I just made, it has grown layer upon layer.

"Tired." It's as honest as I can be right now.

"You should try to get some rest. I'll wake you when we get to the garage." A generous offer. Tempting too. But I still don't know him well enough. Just because I'm betting on him for help, it doesn't mean I trust him.

It's a good excuse to avoid conversation though, so I lean my head against the window and close my eyes. I tuck a hand under my thigh and pinch myself every so often to keep from drifting off.

When he parks the car, I stir, ready to be underground and as far from my old life as possible. He offers to carry my bag as we trudge through the undergrowth. I tighten my fingers around its strap and decline.

Inside, he lets me go down the elevator on my own this time. I savor my last moment alone as the box click, click, clicks its way to the floor below. From here on out, I'll have to be on guard. I step forward and look around.

Ian is not anywhere in sight. Must be sleeping.

Lucky.

I listen as the elevator makes its ascent and then travels back.

"Let's get a room ready for you." Jace says when he appears. He takes my hand as he walks by. "Come with me."

He leads me to the hallway, and I slide my fingers free. He stalls, but only for a microsecond before continuing. "It's this one." He opens one of the doors in the long hallway, revealing a square room with a quilted bed. "You can stay here. The door locks from the inside. Next down the hall is the bathroom." He leads me one room over to show me. Ducking to open the cabinet beneath the sink, he pulls out a boxed toothbrush. "There's toothpaste behind the mirror. Do you need anything right now?"

I take him in. The eagerness to help, the concern. It seems genuine. But I can't figure out why he should care so much. He wants to find his sister, of course, but he seems more focused on... me.

"Time in the bathroom would be great, actually." I move past him onto the tiled floor and drop my bag. The wetness between my thighs has been growing. How long has it been since I changed my pad?

"Okay. I'll leave you alone. Call out if you need anything." With that, he heads deeper into the hallway, and I shut the door, leaning my forehead against the wooden frame. I'm here. I'm really here, and no one from New Harper knows.

One breath. In. Out.

There's a small knock. I steel myself and open the door again, but no one is there. When I step forward to peer around the doorway, my foot hits something soft. A pile of clothes with a note on top.

In case you needed something to sleep in. They're clean. Thank you for coming.

I take the pile into the bathroom and twist the lock. A soft t-shirt and flannel pants. Large. Most likely these are Jace's. It feels a little too personal handling his pajamas. But rifling through my bag produces no pajamas of my own. I was in such a rush, I forgot to grab a pair. A sniff of my own shirt tells me I reek of sweat. All the anxiety leaking out of my body, I suppose. I grimace. I'm tempted to take a shower, but I can't bring myself to get fully naked in a house with two strangers.

Instead, I drop my coat and ditch my shirt and pants for the offered clothes. Relief passes through me when I see own pants aren't stained. I dig through my bag to find the box of pads and replace mine carefully, tossing the soiled one in the trash. As I wash my hands, I remember how inviting the bed looked, feeling a strange gratitude to be here. Everything in my life has turned upside down, but somehow, I've gained a purpose. I find the toothpaste and brush my teeth, willing the act to make the rest of me feel clean. Hoisting my bag and my coat up from the floor, I grip the doorknob.

One breath. In. Out.

I turn the handle and rush into the next room. I close and lock the bedroom door, my heart hammering. A high-backed wooden chair rests in the corner at the foot of the bed. Perfect. I grab it and prop it under the doorknob. Then I rest my bag against the bottom of the door for good measure. No doubt Jace and Ian are strong enough to break through the barricade. The extra second it will give me if they try is what will allow me to sleep. Next, I need something to defend myself. A lamp squats on the wooden table by the bed. I pick it up to test the weight. The base is heavy. It will do.

With safety measures in place, the pressure in my chest releases a bit. I catch my reflection in a mirror and turn to look. The baggy short sleeves reach my elbows and the pant legs pool around my feet, reminding me how small I am. How vulnerable.

I crawl under the covers and curl up tight. I'm too tired to let fear keep me awake. In seconds, I drift into the quiet dark.

THE GRASS SWAYS IN the breeze, between the toes of girls in long white cotton gowns. Twelve girls stand in a circle in the meadow. One tall woman paces around it, looking at each face, her fiery curls dancing about her head. She stops in front of a girl with long dark hair and dirty sneakers. The woman assesses the girl and smiles.

MY HEAD LURCHES UPRIGHT. Disoriented, I process the quilt, the chair against the door, then remember I'm in the cabin. I dig my phone from the coat abandoned on the floor next to the bed. It's past 9:00 a.m.

That was her again. Vanessa. I doubt it would be helpful to state that she is in a random meadow somewhere. Still, I should share the new dream with Jace and Ian.

I toe out of the bed, scoot the chair, and slip into the hallway. A dim light emanates from the kitchen, and another shines down the hall. I head toward the open door, hesitating before poking my head inside.

Jace's torso is slumped onto a desk, head resting on a pile of papers. Black pencils lie scattered all over the surface.

Papers plaster the wall above him as well. I squint, not wanting to move closer and wake him. The papers are drawings. Faces.

They look like me.

The scuff of feet against the floor makes me turn my head back to the hallway. Ian approaches quietly.

"Hi." I whisper. I'm unsure of what to say to him. So far all he's done is tell me that I've been manipulated my whole life.

"Hi," he replies. "I wanted to make sure someone was around to help you if you woke up. Jace was in rough shape, so I told him to hit the sack." He lifts an arm and scratches the back of his head. "Want some food? I make a decent egg scramble."

"Um, sure." My gaze drifts to the wall of portraits.

He tracks the movement. "I'll explain all that. C'mon." Ian leads the way to the kitchen and moves a chair from the dining table to the counter. He motions for me to sit, then proceeds to grab a bowl of eggs before placing a pan on the stove. "I told you we all process the dreams differently," he begins. "Jace draws. He found he can recall the dreams better if he draws out everything he saw as soon as he comes to."

I sit in the chair, trying to keep up with the barrage of words as I rub the sleep from my eyes. There were more than a few drawings of me on that wall. "He did mention he's had dreams about me. Has that been going on long?" I trace the nail bed of my thumb with the nail of my forefinger.

Ian snorts. "Only about three years. I almost didn't believe him when he came home and told me he saw you in person. He sees you so often, I figured it was a waking-dream. But here you are."

At this, he turns to look at me, sobering. "Jace isn't wrong. We could use your help if you really did see Vanessa, but you shouldn't feel obligated to help us. This might get dangerous, and it isn't your fight." He squints at me, then approaches and lifts a hand near my chin. "May I?"

My breath catches in my chest, but I give a slight nod. He uses my chin to turn my head to the side, taking a closer look at my cheek and lip, his eyes tracing the injuries down my neck. I really should apply some makeup to cover up the damage. "Looks like danger might not be a new thing for you. It doesn't look infected. You cleaned it, I assume?" He straightens, crossing his arms over his chest. Are these guys germaphobes?

My mind goes back to Sophia and her cottage. "Yes, it was cleaned." The troubled expression he wears makes me wonder what he would look like if he could see the rest of my injuries. "And I did see her. I saw her again before I woke up. She was in a meadow surrounded by other girls and a red-haired woman. I didn't recognize where. It didn't seem like anywhere around here." I've hiked enough of the surrounding area for me to recognize New Harper's woods. "I'm worried about her. Something about the whole situation seemed off."

Ian's eyes grow wide at my words. He bounds across the room to the coffee table and picks up a journal and pen. When he returns, he is already scribbling something. "The last time you saw her, what did you say happened?"

"She was running through the woods. She looked dazed. I made a noise, and she turned, as if she heard me." Ian's eyes snap to mine.

"Is that normal? Do you usually interact that way in your dreams, where you can affect something?" His fingers are limp now, the pen nearly toppling out of them.

"Not always, but sometimes yes."

When I was twelve, I had a recurring dream where I'd sit on a hill surrounded by butterflies. They'd land on my fingers. A purple one even landed on my nose once. Whenever I'd wake up from that particular dream, I'd find my mom — Audrey — running around the house calling my name. When I'd come to her, she'd cry and say she couldn't find me, that I'd been gone. A few visits to another psychiatrist made her assume I was playing hide and seek while sleepwalking. That she hadn't found my hiding spot in her searches. Something about my subconscious craving for childhood.

But I always woke up in my bed.

Ian interrupts the memory. "How long does it usually take? For your dreams to come true?"

"It depends. Sometimes it takes months, even years. Some never happen. But other times, I find out that what I saw already happened, like I was watching it in real time. These dreams with your sister, they feel more like that. Like I'm there." I sniff the air, smoke tinging my nostrils.

Ian rushes to the pan and takes it off the heat. He turns to me, eggs forgotten.

"We believe Vanessa's disappearance has something to do with Commissioner Copeland. She's not the first one to go missing. We need to search his office, but so far, we haven't managed to bypass security. I haven't found an opening. I mean, it's amazing you've seen her, but a redhead in a meadow isn't enough to go on. We need more information."

A pit forms in my stomach. I should have known escape was too much to ask for.

Hope wasn't made for me.

Copeland's claws are in me too deep.

I think about Vanessa's face. She's just a kid. She has people who care about her. If I can't help myself, I can at least try to help her.

"I can get in."

Ian purses his lips. "What do you mean?"

"I know the commissioner. I can get into his office."

Fifteen

"THANK YOU, LAYLA. YES. Tell the commissioner I look forward to working with him as well." My hands shake as I end the call. I close my eyes.

One breath. In. Out.

"I don't like this." Jace's words break through my anxiety. He sits on the couch, elbows on his knees. His hands form a fist against his mouth.

He tried to talk Ian out of the idea for an hour when he woke up. Insisted there must be an option that doesn't involve my interacting with Copeland. They were in the other room, but I overheard.

And the truth is he's probably right. If it were only about me, I would want to run as far from Copeland as possible. Ian is right too. Vanessa is on her own, and if Copeland is to blame, then she needs any help I can offer her. Deeper than that though, the thing that solidified my decision, is that I need answers too. If I want to leave New Harper, I need to uncover everything I can about Hazelgrove.

Escape.

It was that word, ringing through my mind, that set my

fingers to the keypad of my phone. Both men rushed out of the hall when they heard me talking with Layla.

Now that the call is over, dread pulls at Jace's shoulders.

"She can get us into his office. We need something to go on, Jace. We can't keep waiting around, hoping for a dream that will point us in the right direction. We need to find V." Ian paces behind the couch. I can see the gears turning in his head. It's obvious that this is the chance he's been waiting for.

"How do you know Commissioner Copeland so well?" Jace focuses on me now.

I inhale a shaky breath. Moves and countermoves. Keep my cards close to my chest but give enough to avoid suspicion. "He's been in my life as long as I can remember."

His eyes bore into mine. "Is he going to hurt you?"

I flinch, not sure how to answer.

He asks again. "If you go through with this internship, is Commissioner Copeland going to harm you?"

I search his eyes now, a flare of anger pricking my chest. I've never told a soul about the nature of the commissioner's relationship to me. But I suppose I'm not doing the best job of hiding my fear. Or my actual injuries, for that matter. "I'll be fine. It's like Ian said, we need to find your sister. This is the best way I can help."

I push myself off the couch and stride to my room. Jace's questions are hitting too close to the mark, and I'm not ready to share that much with him. Besides, I don't want an audience for my next call.

Copeland's assistant told me the internship is contingent

upon my resignation from my other job. I have to call Marshall. And I don't want to do it.

I close the door and pace the room, my knuckles white around the plastic of my phone. It shouldn't be this hard. He's just the man who employed me.

But it's more than that, and I know it.

I have to be fast. Get it over with.

I sink into the mattress, my thumb hovering over the keys.

Just dial the number.

I press each button carefully before finally landing on the green call button.

One breath. In. Out.

I press it to my ear, and it rings. Twice. Then beeps. I quickly hit the red button. Quitting over voicemail would be disrespectful. Relief melts over me, the tightness in my abdomen easing. Then I notice the warmth between my legs.

It takes all of a moment for me to cross through both doorways into the bathroom and turn the lock. I pull the door to make sure it's secure. Once I'm certain, I take my seat on the toilet.

Why do I keep forgetting my bleed? This pad is dyed a deep burgundy, not a speck of white left. And of course I didn't bring my box in with me.

I lean over, hoping there's something under the sink I can use. From what I've seen, these guys are well prepared in their sanctuary. And there is no way I'm calling out for one of them to bring me anything. Not while I'm in this position. The edge of the cabinet bites my arm as I push things around on the shelf.

With a sigh of relief, I pull out a box identical to the one from Marshall's store. It looks fairly new, though opened. There's one left. I'll replace it later.

I clean myself up and situate the pad and my pants, standing to wash my hands. A smear of blood darkens my fingers. When I notice it, a prickle climbs the nape of my neck. The pad box, silent and still, sits upon the counter's edge, yet it dominates the space, screaming at me.

Hazelgrove.

Escape.

If only I could decipher the deeper meaning of the words. I flip on the faucet and let the water wash over my bloody fingers. A sharp sensation courses from the crown of my head to my feet, and the world falls out from under me.

I blink.

When my eyes open, the freefall halts. I see dense trees under a dark night sky. Cold, soft mud squelches beneath my bare feet. A puddle of water covers my skin, seeping into the too-long legs of Jace's borrowed pants faster than the panic seeping into my chest.

I know where I am.

Laughter trills in the distance, and I strain my ears trying to key in on where it's coming from. When I feel certain, I depart, attempting to step quietly. The edge of the treeline forces me to slow. The voices are louder now. I flatten myself against a large trunk, peering around it.

The scene in front of me mimics the one I saw before. Girls in nightgowns, facing one another in a large circle.

The red-haired woman is pacing around them again. I'm too preoccupied searching the faces of every dark-haired girl to pay attention to her.

I spot Vanessa at the far end of the meadow from where I hide. She stands swaying and chanting with the rest of the group. How do I reach her without anyone noticing? If I can draw her away from the group, I can explain her brothers sent me, and then... and then we'll both be stuck here. I retreat from the scene, letting the tree block it from view. I have no idea where we are, how I got here, or how to go back. Even if I can get Vanessa's attention, I can't get her home. I sink down, my back sliding along the rough bark of the tree behind me.

One breath. In. Out.

"Hello."

My head snaps to the whisper, bringing me nose to nose with a woman and her sparkling copper eyes. I lurch backward, scraping my arm against the tree as I maneuver around it, stumbling on my hands and heels to put distance between us. It's the red-haired woman. Her knowing smile holds no surprise at finding me here.

"Come with me," she says, nodding over her shoulder. "You can meet the others." She turns and walks back into the meadow, the hem of her white dress floating over the grass. She expects me to follow. She knows I have nowhere to run.

I stand and dust myself off. Glancing behind me, I'm met by the darkness of the forest. No knowing what lies within. With no other options, I approach the meadow, leaving the cover of the trees.

The other girls hardly notice, now milling about and speaking to one another. They break off into groups and exit into the forest. I've lost track of Vanessa in the shuffle.

The woman sits elegantly in the center of the grass. "Take a seat." She motions for me to join her. I lower myself to the ground, but I keep my mouth shut. I'll let her do the talking. "What brings you to Hazelgrove?" she asks, an easy smile gracing her lips, though her eyes are like a hawk's, ready to dive upon its prey.

Hazelgrove.

My heart ticks faster, but I remain silent, watching her. Her cotton nightgown is simple and unadorned, but her beauty is undeniable. Striking. "You're welcome to leave. The women here are all recruits. Of course, if you need somewhere to stay, we can always use another volunteer." Now she waits, eyebrow raised. A challenge?

If I want answers, I'm going to have to ask the questions. "Volunteer for what? And where did you say we are?"

Her smile grows. "This is Hazelgrove. We are a refuge for all women and girls who seek safety. Do you seek safety?" Her mouth purses at this, head angling to one side, considering me. "You do, don't you?" She stands, gown twirling around her ankles. "I know it is difficult, trusting after someone has used you. Would you like to see our operation?"

Everything in me wants to run in the other direction. What she's suggesting is too good to be true. An escape. Safety. There must be some other angle she's hiding. But I know it would be pointless to try to leave. Maybe if I go with her, I'll be able to find Vanessa again. I stand, give a small nod.

"Excellent." The woman loops her arm through mine and guides us forward. We exit the meadow onto a path in the dirt, trees surrounding us once again. I hear water rushing, growing louder the farther we walk. Soon I can make out a river cutting through the forest, the path following it for a length before it turns. "We have a settlement here. Every volunteer pitches in to ensure all residents have a place to sleep, food to eat, clothes to wear. We care for the grove, and it cares for us. Hazelgrove is a special place. A haven."

The path opens onto a corridor of buildings, all blended seamlessly into the greenery. Between the buildings lies a courtyard of sorts. Girls tend a few fires. The center holds a well constructed from stones, with a rope suspending a wooden pail.

"How far outside New Harper is this Hazelgrove?" I offer the question, hoping to glean some sense of our whereabouts. "I can't imagine the commissioner would have sanctioned this."

"Ah, you are from New Harper. And you know Erebus." Something flashes in her copper eyes. "Yes, I should have seen it in you." The woman appraises me again, tight curls bouncing around her shoulders. "That man is a monster. Though I expect I do not need to explain that to you. I can assure you, we are nowhere near his little project. Come with me." She walks briskly across the settlement, and I hurry to follow.

Soon we're back in the thick of the pine branches. I struggle to keep sight of the red hair between the green foliage. She disappears completely, and my feet crunch over dried needles as I push aside a large branch. When I step forward, heat and blinding light overtake me.

I throw my arm over my face to block it out. My pulse skyrockets. A cool hand touches my shoulder.

"Open your eyes. They'll adjust." I blink at the woman now standing before me on a hard floor of baked sand. Ahead of us waits a wasteland, reaching all the way to the horizon. "Turn around." I turn, and behind me glows a curtain of light. Gauzy and almost not there at all.

"What is this? How did we get here?" I know I'm not sleeping. This isn't one of my dreams, and that terrifies me. Before I was lost, but now I'm isolated.

"As I explained, Hazelgrove is a special place. It is a refuge. One that men can never infiltrate." She's pacing now, fingers skimming the surface of the barrier, light rippling at her touch, creating a snaking river of glowing white in the air.

"How is that possible? How is any of this possible?" Magic curtains. Transporting between worlds in the blink of an eye. This shouldn't be real.

She comes toward me and offers her hand. I'm afraid of what will happen if I refuse her, so I take it. She leads me again through the curtain, and now that I'm paying attention, I can see the moment between the change. Light and dark, hot and cold, hard and soft. All meet at the filmy passageway. A seamless transition.

She takes hold of my hands in hers and looks at me with shimmering eyes. "It is possible because we are women. We are portals, and we create portals."

I stare at her. "Portals? What does that mean? Portals to where?"

"To new life." She takes a breath, pondering her next words. "Take birth, for instance. A new life passes through the mother, from a realm inside the woman, to an exterior realm. She is a portal for her child."

The base of my head aches. I shake it, trying to relieve the pain. "What are you talking about?" She's speaking nonsense.

Realization dawns on her face. "You're from New Harper," she says, hushed. Her grip on my hand tightens. "Come. I will show you." She drags me back through the forest. My body wants to shut down. This is all too much.

Soon we're striding on the cleared dirt path between the buildings, but she doesn't let up. She marches over to a door and knocks, one hand still gripping mine. Another woman opens the door.

"Demelza," she greets the woman, smiling. "What can I do for you?"

"How is Alta doing? Is she awake?" Demelza asks.

"Yes, she's doing well, just getting ready for a walk. Would you like to see her?" She steps back, gesturing for us to enter.

"Thank you, Eva." Demelza pats her shoulder. We pass through the foyer into a small room full of handmade furniture. Another woman sits here, swaying in a rocking chair. All seems normal until my eyes land on her stomach. It bulges against her dress as if a large boulder is stuck inside.

"Alta, how are you?" Demelza releases me from her grip and moves forward to embrace the woman. Alta smiles. Using one arm to cradle her stomach, her other braces the arm of the rocking chair.

She hoists herself up and hugs Demelza, then notices me and smiles again.

"Hello," she says. "I don't believe we've met. I'm Alta." She immediately wraps me in a hug as well, her large belly pressing against mine. It's solid, but softer than I expected. "What is your name, dear?"

I've never met someone so open, so inviting. Her whole face radiates with her wide smile.

"Sariah."

"Oh, that's a lovely name." Alta turns to Demelza. "What can I do for you both?"

Demelza settles herself onto a rug on the floor. "Sariah has never met a pregnant mother. I wondered if you'd be willing to show her the baby?"

Baby. The word Jace and Ian used.

"Oh, of course. Come, dear, let's sit." Alta bids me to join Demelza on the rug. She lowers herself to the floor and begins pulling up her dress. Fine white lines cover her tanned legs and belly, like her skin is ready to rip apart. The ache in my head grows. I look at her stomach, round and protruding away from the rest of her body.

"Ah!" I brace my face with my hands as the searing reaches my brows.

"Sariah, I know this does not make sense, but you must open your eyes. Your mind has been held back from you, but you can break that hold. Focus." I don't understand Demelza's words, but I will do whatever it takes to stop the pain. I force my eyes open.

"Oh, she's kicking!" Alta exclaims. She grabs one of my

hands and holds it against her belly. Something from inside it pushes against my palm. Instantly, the pain breaks like a window shattering. It's gone, and a strange sense of space unfurls in my mind.

"What was that?" I croak. It was undeniably alive, but how could something be alive inside her stomach?

Alta laughs. "Well, it was the baby, of course. I haven't named her yet, but I've got ideas. She'll be ready to join the world soon."

I nod despite my confusion. My mind is so quiet now. Eerie.

Demelza lays a gentle hand on my knee. "I am going to ask you a question, Sariah. You may find it a bit troubling, but it is going to help things make sense." I meet her eyes, and she continues. "Where do people come from?"

Ian asked me this before. I still don't know.

"People join New Harper as children," Demelza explains. "Usually around ten years old. However, those individuals entered the world first as small and helpless humans. Their bodies were each formed inside of a woman, like Alta here. The woman carried them as they grew and developed until they were ready. At which point, they exited the woman's body. That is how life is made."

I stare at Alta's exposed stomach. "But how does it get in there? I've lived around women my whole life, and I've never seen this." I point to where I felt the baby move, then stand and walk the room, back and forth, unable to stop my feet. My fingers dig into my nail beds, cuticles tearing at the edges. I can't deny what Demelza said, what Ian said. I've never seen a child younger than ten, and I've never stopped to question where they came from.

Demelza comes over to stop me. "This is a lot to take in. Let me find a room for you. You can stay here, and I will teach you everything Erebus has hidden from you."

She calls him Erebus.

He's a friend, sweetheart, you should call him by his first name. Audrey's voice chants in my head.

When Demelza says his name, it's saturated with malice, but she uses it all the same. I can't overlook that. Turning on my heel, I run through the foyer to the front door, then grip the knob and yank it open. I sprint for the trees.

Demelza isn't far behind.

Sixteen

The rushing of water meets my ears again. Demelza's fingers claw my forearm as I stumble into the river. Her nails break my skin as I tear my arm away, falling toward the water. They gouge deep into my flesh. "Get off!" I shout. I just want to go home. An abrupt tugging in my gut knocks me even more off balance.

I land on something hard. My hands splay behind me to catch myself, rough cement grating my palms.

My arm sears, and I roll over, clutching it against my body, the pain ringing in my ears.

One breath. In. Out.

I look down and see a huge, bleeding gash in my forearm. The rushing of the water is gone. Instead, a soft mist of rain teases the gray sidewalk. Covering my wound with the bottom of my shirt — Jace's shirt — I look up to find the side of Marshall's store.

Slowly, I inch my way to stand. Inside is dark, so I cup my good hand over my eyes to peek through the window. I can just make out the clock. 2:00 a.m. How can it be that late? I could not possibly have been gone longer than an hour. I struggle to keep my breath steady.

No one occupies the street, so I stumble on shaky legs to the back door, running my fingers over the red and brown ridges of the wall.

"Please still be here," I mutter. Next to the doorway, I wiggle the false brick free. My wet hand slips against the rough surface, struggling to grip it. Finally, it gives. I slide it out and point the backside up. The golden key glints at me from the hollow of the brick.

A sigh falls from my lips. "Thank you, Marshall."

My left arm is useless, so I set the brick on the ground and dig out the key. I hold it between my teeth while I replace the brick. Then I unlock the back door and slip inside, switching on the light.

Marshall's desk sits littered with papers and supplies. I can feel the blood dripping from my shirt now, dizziness taking over my vision for a moment. I need to close the wound. I hobble to the wall and pull down the white plastic case.

Prying it open reveals a handful of small bandages. I must have used all the gauze and sterile pads on Jace. Collapsing into the chair at the desk and struggling to keep my eyes from drifting shut, I open each of the drawers. Pens, rubber bands, scissors, shift logs, duct tape, a wall stapler, Marshall's stash of booze. Dismal options. But I know what I have to do.

My hand lands on the stapler, which I push aside to grab the scissors and duct tape. Then I pull out a half-empty bottle of vodka. The trash bin scrapes along the floor as I drag it from the side of the desk and set it in front of me. My shirt is thoroughly soaked in blood now. I don't want to pull my left arm from my stomach until I must, so I cross my left ankle over my knee. The scissors shake in my fingers as I take them to Jace's flannel pajama pants, first removing the mud-soaked ends, which plop wet on the tile, then cutting off a wide strip of the cleaner fabric. I use my teeth to rip a few strips of duct tape and attach the ends to the edge of the desk.

One breath. In. Out.

I pull the cap off the vodka and peel my left arm away from me, setting it over the trash bin. I tip the bottle, sucking in another breath as the alcohol stings the wound. Once I've doused the whole thing, I grab the strip of cloth and press it over the laceration. Liquid seeps through the fabric immediately, red pushing up in the cracks between my fingers. I hurry to secure the cloth with duct tape, then press it back against my body, trying to maintain pressure.

My head spins. Lights flash across my vision.

Two quiet knocks sound at the back exit. I wait silently, watching the handle turn. The door inches open slowly.

I can't identify the face that appears before it leans back and hisses, "She's here!" The door opens fully, and Ian rushes around the desk, taking in my makeshift infirmary. Jace follows, a single second behind, eyes wide.

An unfamiliar relief floods my chest, but as my muscles relax, the pain rises full force, refusing to be ignored.

"Are you okay to move?" Ian asks. I nod, swallowing the bile in my throat. "Okay. Let's clean this up and get out before anyone finds us. We'll get you back to the cabin, and you can tell us what happened." He starts putting things back into drawers. Grabbing the soiled trash bin, he removes the liner full of bloody vodka and replaces it with a fresh one from the roll at the bottom of the bin.

It's not exactly where I found things, but Marshall won't notice.

It takes Jace a full minute to start moving. His face is drained of color when he comes around the desk and kneels beside me. "Can I carry you? The car is right outside."

"I can walk." I lean forward, rising to stand, and topple over. Jace's hands are faster than my momentum, pulling me upright and leaning me against him. I try to take a step with the added support, but my vision spots.

"I'm going to pick you up," Jace grunts as he readjusts, pulling my knees up with one arm to cradle me against his chest. The world turns black.

I WAKE IN A cold sweat. The details of Jace's cabin come into focus slowly. Soft snoring rumbles to my right.

Jace.

He sleeps in a chair beside the bed, his head on his folded arms leaning on the mattress next to me. His hand curls limp around my fingers. I watch him as things come into focus. His shoulders rise and fall slowly. His dark hair sticks up in places, as if he'd been running his hands through it. The weariness under his eyes is softened with sleep. I become aware of the heat of his skin against mine, and I slip my fingers away carefully. He starts and sits upright, looking around until his blue eyes land on me.

"You're awake," he breathes. In a flash, he consumes my

whole field of vision. "How are you feeling?" He's so close, hovering over me, stroking my hair back from my face with a gentle hand. He looks at me with rapt attention, like nothing else matters. I attempt to sit so I can edge away from his touch, but spots dance across the room. He helps me lower down, then retreats a step. "I'm sorry," he mutters. "I don't mean to keep doing that. Touching you. It's hard to separate what's in my head from what's in front of me." He turns and paces, shaking his head at himself, running a hand through his dark mussed hair. I hear him whisper, "Idiot."

The word pricks something in my chest. Guilt?

"What do you mean?" I ask. Of course I've noticed how much he touches me, but I've also noticed that he always lets go if I pull away. I can't say the same for other men I've met. He stops and looks at me, like he didn't hear what I said. "What do you mean?" I repeat, "What's in your head?"

He takes a breath, then grabs the chair he'd been sleeping in and drags it a foot away from the bed. When he sits, his gaze is still too familiar, like he knows me better than he does.

"I've had the dreams since I was little. Not too many, but here and there. My parents would track them until they disappeared. Anyway, three years ago I started having dreams more often. A lot more often. And they were all about one person."

I remember what Ian said in the kitchen. "Me," I whisper.

Jace nods. "I want you to know I don't expect anything from you. We've just met, right? Just a few days ago. But I feel like I've known you for years, that we've known each other, that we..." he breaks off, looks at the floor. "But those are just dreams. This is real, you, right now, and you're scared, and I keep scaring you." He buries his face in his hands.

I weigh his words in my mind. He's seen a different version of me in his dreams. A version of me that is with him, beyond our current arrangement, to find Vanessa. A version of me that he feels he can touch freely. I doubt that could ever be real.

"Did they come true? When you were young, did your dreams ever come true?" I wait for him to look up.

When he does, his eyes trace my lips. "Always."

That puzzles me. "It's not your fault," I say. "It's not your fault I'm scared. You've done so much to help me." My brain catches up with everything that has happened up until now. "How did you know where I was? At the store? How did you find me?" They got there so quickly. And my phone was still here, so they couldn't have used the GPS.

"I had a vision. You were hurt, sitting on the street. I knocked on the bathroom door, but you wouldn't answer. I couldn't hear anything inside but the sink running, so I forced the door open, and you were gone. We jumped into the car and drove as fast as we could. Ian and I spent all day and night driving through New Harper. I was positive you were by the store in the vision, so eventually we parked near there and waited. When we saw the light flick on, we just hoped it was you we were following in there. I'm glad we found you when we did. You lost a lot of blood."

At this, I turn my attention to my left arm. My duct tape and pajama bandage are gone, replaced with a thick gauze wrap. It makes me think of Sophia and her cabin full of remedies.

"You fainted before we reached the car, and you haven't woken up until now. The wound was still bleeding out, so we cleaned it. We were able to use bandages to hold the skin together. But it's deep. We really should put in stitches."

My head falls back onto the pillow. With my attention drawn to it, my arm throbs with pain, like something is pressing on a bruise from the inside. I'm scared to move it.

"Why is everyone hiding out in these woods basically a doctor?" I ask, more to the ceiling than to Jace.

"What do you mean? Were you with someone last night?" He asks.

"Oh, my goodness, Jace!" I almost spring out of the bed before thinking better of it. "I found her. I saw her. I was there with Vanessa. I used the bathroom and then somehow, I was in the meadow. The dream I told Ian about, with the red-haired woman. I talked to her. Her name is Demelza. She's been recruiting girls and women to live in Hazelgrove, and there was a baby inside of a woman's stomach, and—" I gasp for a breath.

"Slow down," Jace tells me. He moves to the doorway. "Just calm down for a second. Ian!" he calls. "Ian, get in here! Sariah found Vanessa!" A trampling sound fills the hallway before Ian skids into the room. He stands at the foot of the bed, bouncing on the balls of his feet. Jace resumes his place in the chair. "Okay, Sariah. Start from the beginning. Tell us everything."

One breath. In. Out.

"I came in here to try calling my boss, but he didn't answer. So I went to the bathroom. I've been so distracted with everything,

I forgot that I'm," I glance between the men, "well, I needed a pad. I forgot to bring one with me, but I found a box under the sink. I took one, but I promise I'll replace it."

"Hold on." Ian raises a hand to stop me. "You found a pad in this bathroom?" He points to the wall shared with the bathroom. I nod. "But we don't keep those there. Feminine supplies are in our parent's room. Vanessa doesn't need them. She doesn't menstruate yet."

I shrug. "They were tucked in the back of the cabinet, behind everything else." Ian and Jace share a glance.

"You don't think—" Ian starts.

"Maybe Vanessa didn't tell us? It's been a few years since Mom disappeared, and I'm not sure how much she told V," Jace replies.

Ian chews his cheek. "Okay. What happened after that?"

"Let me think." I piece the events of last night in the correct order. "I washed my hands and then I was in the forest. I heard the girls, I found the meadow, and Demelza found me. The woman from the dream. I'm not sure how I returned either. I fell into a river and then I was at the shop. It doesn't make any sense." I rack my brain, trying to remember, straining to make sense of it all.

"The bathroom light was on when V went missing," Ian says to himself. "She was home when we turned in for bed, but vanished in the morning with zero sign of where she'd gone."

More of my conversation with Demelza enters my mind. "What does the word pregnant mean to you?" I look at them both.

"Vanessa's not pregnant, is she? I swear if that snake

Copeland got our little sister pregnant—" Rage floods Ian's face.

"Hold on," Jace diffuses his brother. "Sariah, why do you ask?"

"There was a woman there. She had a huge stomach, with a baby inside. I felt it move." The moment replays in my mind. So strange. "Hold on." I register what Ian just said. "What do you mean that Copeland could have gotten your sister pregnant? How would he put a baby inside of her?"

Terror grips me at the idea that something could be living inside me right now without my knowing. I would know, wouldn't I?

Tendrils of pain ensnare my arm. I clutch it to my chest, but the pressure doesn't help. The cut burns under the bandages. Jace's eyes are round with fear as I cry out.

"What is that?" Ian asks him.

I look at the infected arm, trying to locate the source of the pain. Dark streaks of green swim through the veins beneath my skin, spreading into my hand. Tears fill my eyes, blurring the sight into an inky mess.

"What do we do?" Ian yells at his brother. He's unsettled. Jace watches, transfixed.

This isn't a normal injury. They're obviously taken aback by it, and I refuse to visit the hospital in town. The memory surfaces in my mind of a makeshift infirmary in a warm cottage.

"Do you know Sophia?" I hiss between labored breaths. Maybe they've crossed paths, both living out here on the edge of town. If anyone would know how to help, something tells me it would be her. They both shake their heads, horror exposing the whites of their eyes.

One breath. In. Out.

Don't let the panic win. Not now.

Sophia is the best option for help.

I think back to her driver, the car, the road leading into town. I could backtrack, right? It wouldn't be far from here.

"We need to get to the car."

SEVENTEEN

MY INCISORS DIG INTO my lower lip.

Pain to drown pain.

Jace drives and Ian sits in the back of the station wagon. I stare ahead out the window, watching for any signs of where the men dropped me. "It was raining the night she found me. But we were able to walk from the street to the cottage. There's a path somewhere past the trees." Speaking is agony.

"Why were you out here alone at night?" Ian asks, leaning forward.

My teeth break my lip, a metallic taste flooding over my tongue. "Ow!" I press my good hand against my mouth. Jace veers off the road and puts the car in park.

"What's wrong?" He looks at the infected arm, but I shake my head.

"It's nothing. Bit my lip. Do you have any water I can drink?" If I don't get this taste out of my mouth, I may vomit. He quickly retrieves a bottle from his door, unscrews it, and hands it to me. I catch sight of the green spreading through my skin and shiver. I may pass out.

My dizziness must be visible, because both Jace and Ian put

their hands on me to hold me upright. I don't have the strength to push them away. I want to find Sophia as soon as possible. Hand shaking, I lift the bottle and take a sip.

Like a rug is ripped out from under me, I'm thrown off balance, my sight going fuzzy before normalizing.

"What just happened?" Ian yells, his hand still gripping my shoulder from the seat behind mine. We're all still sitting in the car. But something is different.

I look out the windshield. Standing next to one of the trees, John waves at us, his cap on his head, an amused smile on his face.

We found it. If he's here, Sophia must be close. I tuck the injured limb to my body and hop out of the car, hurrying towards the driver.

"She's waiting for you." John says as soon as I'm within earshot. He nods towards the woods to his right. Jace and Ian have already caught up with me. I don't waste time on introductions or explanations. I break into a lop-sided run, letting my adrenaline carry me down the path.

The cottage comes into view. The front door is wide open, and the smell wafting from it makes my mouth water in spite of the pain. "This is it!" I call over my shoulder.

Jace is closer than I thought, and he puts a hand on my arm, stopping me short. "Sariah, wait. What are you talking about? The only thing here is more trees." I turn to see them both looking at me expectantly.

"You don't see the cottage? It's right there." I turn back to it, and sure enough the circular home sits between the foliage, white smoke curling from the chimney. They don't move. "All right, you guys wait here. I'll go in." Jace opens his mouth to retort, but I'm tired of the confusion, my arm is screaming at me, and I'm willing to bet that if anyone has answers, it's Sophia.

I stomp to the front door. Before I can burst through the entrance, a voice calls from inside. "Come in, Sariah, I'm getting the food plated for you." Taken aback, I inch past the doorway. Sophia is ladling soup from a large stockpot into bowls and putting them on the table. "You will have to assist the boys. They will not be able to enter by themselves," she tells me as she takes a knife to a loaf of bread.

"How do I do that?" She's not surprised at our appearance.

"Hold their hands. If they desire to accompany you, they will be able to."

"Right." I turn around and trudge painfully to Jace and Ian. "She's home. She said I have to bring you in, so..." I awkwardly position myself between them and hold out my hands. The injured one shakes. "We'll have to walk in together." Jace gingerly balances my bandaged hand in his. Ian hesitates but takes hold of my other outstretched hand. As soon as they are touching me, they both stiffen.

"I see it now," Jace says. Ian murmurs in agreement.

By the time we're over the threshold, Sophia stands by the set table. "Come in, take a seat."

I drop their hands, and we each take a chair. The delicious aroma of the meal has me salivating, but we didn't come for food. I need help.

"Sariah," the woman addresses me as she takes the seat across from mine. "What do you want to know?" She seems relaxed. Her long dark hair cascades over her back.

Everything.

Instead of answering, I raise my arm. The green tendrils are turning black, overtaking my fingertips. The pain grows harsher every second.

Her eyes widen, but she wastes no time, turning back to her kitchen and grabbing jars and dishes and bundles of leaves that she brings back and sets in the center of the table. She stands beside me, taking my arm in her sure hands, unwrapping the binding, exposing the wound. A soft click of her tongue, then she lays my arm on the table and cups a small bowl in her palm. With a finger, she scoops a bit of paste from the bowl and rubs it over the gash. I stiffen, expecting pain, but relax when there is none. My eyes must be playing tricks. Dishes clatter as Jace and Ian knock into the table for a better look.

As Sophia's finger glides over my skin, the wound closes, not even leaving behind a scar. She reaches for a bundle of green leaves and a box of matches. Flames light the top of the bundle for a moment before she blows them out and swirls the smoke around my arm. The inky trails dissipate, fading until there's nothing left but the normal blue and purple of my veins.

When she's finished, she takes a clean napkin from the table and runs it over my skin to remove the goop. I inspect my arm. It's as smooth as ever, with no sign of injury. Most miraculously though, the pain has vanished.

"How did you do that?" Jace asks, leaning in to get a clear view.

"Who did this to your arm?" Sophia speaks to me.

"A woman named Demelza." My answer is a challenge. How much does this woman know? My whole life may be a lie, but someone must know the truth.

Something crosses her expression. "How is Demelza?"

"You know her?"

"Yes. At least I used to. She closed herself off from me years ago. She was hurting." Sophia's eyes speak of wistful memories.

Ian interjects. "We need to find our sister. She went missing. Sariah found her with this woman, and we need to bring her back home."

Sophia waves the smoking leaves in front of her, like she's batting away pesky thoughts. "It's best we start from the beginning, so there is no confusion. First, sit. Eat." She gathers the items from the table and returns them to the kitchen while we resume our seats.

"Should we eat it?" Jace asks me quietly.

I look again at the food. The deep purple soup wafts rich, warm notes of herbs. If Sophia had wanted to hurt me, she could have abandoned me naked on the street.

"Yes, let's eat." The bread touches my tongue, and I realize how famished I am. Once I've taken a bite, the others don't have any problem digging in.

Sophia joins us again, and I start with what I know is true. I may be hungry, but I won't waste precious time. "We have dreams."

She nods.

"Dreams that come true in real life." She waits silently for me to continue.

"Their sister disappeared. I did too. I blinked and appeared in a different place. Then we come here, and they can't see your cabin, but I can. What is going on? How is any of this possible?" I struggle to keep my composure. Tears form in my eyes. I'm so exhausted. Not only from these past few days of late nights and world-altering revelations, but from a whole life of feeling lost in my own skin.

"Last time we spoke, I told you something about yourself. Do you remember?" She watches me, patient.

I try to think back. "You said I underestimate myself."

Sophia nods. "You believe you lack the power to create change or consequence, but creation is in your very nature."

Her words stir something in my heart. But it's overshadowed by hopeless confusion.

"Do you mean pregnancy, like, babies?" I'm not sure I'm following. Jace and Ian sit still, watching our exchange, no longer eating, not making a sound. I hear the wind rustling the leaves outside before she answers me.

"Bearing life into physical form is a great feat of creation. But it is not all. You said you went somewhere. Would you like to share more about that?" My story hasn't fazed her yet. Maybe this will.

"I was in Hazelgrove. A woman named Demelza talked to me, told me I could join their settlement. She has women and girls there. But I still don't understand where it is or how I arrived there or how I returned. She showed me something. There was some sort of barrier around her forest. She said it kept them safe."

"Sariah, what do you want to know?" Sophia asks, intent. I stop and consider the question. What do I want?

"I want our sister back," Ian interjects. Jace kicks him under the table.

"Sariah, do you share that desire?" The woman keeps her eyes trained on me.

"I want to be safe. And I want Vanessa to be safe. I think she'll be safer with her brothers than with a stranger." I remain undecided about Demelza's true intentions.

"Then what you need are eyes to see clearly and a desire to go. Everything else is already inside you. Now please eat before it gets cold." She excuses herself, disappearing into another room.

Jace's eyes are on me. I meet them with my own but say nothing. His hand slides an inch over the table toward mine, but he stops, turning to his food instead. His shoulders sag as he chews a bite, weariness clear in their slope. Ian shovels spoonfuls into his mouth.

I push my seat back and follow Sophia.

Through a doorway, she stands near a bursting bookshelf, looking over the spines of heavy tomes.

"I need your help." I admit. "I don't know what I'm supposed to do to find Vanessa again."

"There is much I could teach you, but I fear retrieving their sister does not allow us much time. Sariah, you will have to find Demelza. Be mindful when passing through veils, or you can expect more injury." She runs a finger over one of the books.

"Veils? So, you know how I got there?" I step closer, eager for any scrap of clarity. "I've only been able to do it by accident. I don't have control over it."

She turns. "Did you utilize light or water when you found Demelza?"

I think about when I blinked into the forest. I was washing my hands. Coming back, I stepped into a river. "Water. I touched water."

She nods. "You're bleeding then." Not a question. I stare at her, desperate to understand. Sophia takes a breath in and out of her nose. "Your flow connects to your life force. Your life force extends eternally, beyond this world. As a woman, you act as a bridge between worlds, which allows you to pass back and forth between them if you so choose. It requires focus. When combined with your life force, water can be a conduit."

I let that sink in. "So, what? I just need to touch water again and I can find Vanessa?" I could go right now, grab her, and bring her home.

"Was someone touching you when you passed back through to your plane?"

I process the question.

"Yes, Demelza grabbed my arm. She was trying to stop me. Is that why it got infected?"

Age peeks through in the lines around Sophia's eyes. She places a gentle hand around my wrist. "Souls must pass through willingly, otherwise complications may occur. If Vanessa does not choose to come with you, forcing her is not worth the risk."

EIGHTEEN

"WHAT MAKES YOU BELIEVE she won't come back with you? Why would she want to stay trapped in some forest with total strangers?" Ian paces his living room like he can speed walk his way out of this dilemma.

I repeat what I've been saying for the past hour. "I only saw her for a few seconds when I went to Hazelgrove. But in every dream I've had, she seems happy to be there." Ian scowls. He's bitter, but I know I'm making sense. "I don't understand why she left you, but Demelza said all the girls are 'recruits.' Presumably, Vanessa volunteered herself. But how could she have known? We need to shift focus to learning anything we can about Demelza. She's luring girls into her world, and we need to find out how. Or why. She knew Commissioner Copeland. She knew about New Harper and the lies. If we can figure out what she's up to, we can convince your sister to leave Hazelgrove and come home."

"But why don't you go back and ask Vanessa now? Maybe she's not as confused as you think. Maybe she doesn't know how to leave. You could show her!" Ian fumes with frustration, but Jace stays quiet on the couch.

"Jace," I try to break the train of thought I see traveling the furrow in his forehead, "what do you think?" Ian and I have been going back and forth on the issue for long enough.

He inhales. "It would be reckless to single Vanessa out while we know so little about how she got there. So far, we know she's in one piece. I don't want to put her in danger unless we have a real plan to help her."

Ian stomps out of the room, into the hallway, and slams his bedroom door.

Jace heaves a weighted sigh. "We'll figure this out," he assures me. "I just wish I knew how she got tangled up in this mess. And how I missed it." His voice trails the last sentence.

How would a young girl end up in Hazelgrove?

Hazelgrove.

The cipher.

The dots start connecting in my head.

"Jace, did you ever let Vanessa go shopping by herself?"

"Never alone, no. She's only twelve. I'm in charge of the shopping. Why?"

It's time to tell him. "Wait here." I retrieve my bag from the room I've been using. The green card and the box hide at the bottom of it, and I dig them out. Then I stop in the bathroom to locate the box under the sink.

I carry all three items to the living room and set them on the coffee table. Jace eyes each of them and raises a brow. "What are those?"

"They're pads," I say. "From the store where I work. I bought these a few days ago." I lift my box in front of me, then raise the other. "And these are the ones I found in your bathroom. It's the same box. You never bought these for your sister?"

He shakes his head. "Come here." Jace stands from the couch and walks down the hallway, leaving me to follow a few strides behind. He halts in front of the doorway at the end of the hall. "This is my parents' room. My mom kept all the medical supplies in a closet in here." He pauses before turning the knob and entering the room, continuing to an attached bathroom. A stale odor fills my nostrils, and I glance quickly around the room before following. Sheets that were likely once white but have taken on a gray hue cover the bed. Random items clutter the tops of dressers. Dust covers the lampshades. This room has remained untouched for some time.

I turn and see Jace open the closet and reach up to one of the top shelves. "These are what my mom kept on hand. She had this big stash of them."

It is a box of pads, but the label is different: *Harper Supply Company*. Harper. Not New Harper. Strange. The faded cardboard bends at my touch. It's likely been sitting here for years.

He sees the difference too. "You think Vanessa bought them?"

I shrug. "You said she hadn't mentioned getting her cycle. Maybe she didn't know where to look for supplies, and was too uncomfortable to ask."

"You think she snuck out? It's miles to the store. She would have needed the car. When would she have left? And wouldn't someone report a child driving around? The cops could have taken her into custody!" The volume of his voice rises with every sentence.

He shoves the old box back on the shelf and throws the cabinet door closed with a smack.

The sound makes me jump. I retreat a few steps, putting distance between us. With his back to me, he presses his hands on either side of the sink, breathing hard, and hangs his head.

I swallow the lump in my throat. "People aren't all that observant. They see what they want to see." I look down, a bitter taste filling my mouth at the truth of the statement. My words are quiet. "She could have waited until you were both asleep and made a quick trip. Unless of course you have a habit of bringing girls back home, then these could be anybody's." The joke is in bad taste, and I wish I could take it back.

Jace chuckles. He actually chuckles.

My cheeks flame.

He turns to face me again. Then his lips turn down, and he takes a slow breath. "You are the only person outside our family who has ever been here. And Vanessa did know how to drive and where to go. I've been teaching her in case of an emergency, and I've been taking her on errands. She told me she felt cooped up, stuck here all the time. But I can't believe she'd go out on her own. We've told her how dangerous it is." He grips the side of the bathroom counter, face falling with a defeated exhale. "What do we do?" His blue eyes swim with worry.

I consider for a moment. "I think I should talk to Marshall."

NINETEEN

"IT'S GOOD TO SEE you, Sariah. I'll admit, I was pretty shocked to get a call from Commissioner Copeland about you." Marshall sits in his desk chair, the mess of papers and pens strewn in front of him. The plastic groans as he leans back.

My heart sinks. "I told him not to call. I wanted to tell you myself." I look at my feet, the toe of my sneaker scraping over the white tile. "If I could keep working here, I would. My personal life has gotten complicated. I had to take the job."

He looks me over, a frown denting the space between his eyebrows. He knows. He knows the commissioner is using me. Sweat forms in my underarms. I have to keep it together.

Marshall sniffs. "Well, we'll miss you. Unfortunately, not many employees share your diligence. Anyway, what brought you by? Did you leave something?" He shuffles around the piles of pages like he'll locate an item of mine in the disarray.

"I have a favor to ask. You still keep security footage of the store, right?" I try to refrain from picking at my nail beds.

"Of course. Why, what happened?" He's already pulling his keys out of his pocket. He opens the desk drawer that holds the drives with old footage.

"I'm looking for someone. A customer, or at least I think she was a customer here. I want to see if she was ever caught on the store's cameras." I don't want to lie to him, but I know I can't tell him the whole truth. The less he knows, the less he'll be at risk. I don't need to get him wrapped up in this conspiracy. My heart races. What if he says no?

"Sariah, you know I can't just give you our security tapes. I really shouldn't even let you watch them. Unless something happened to you, then of course I would make an exception." He doesn't close the drawer. He just waits for me to elaborate. He must think there's something else on those tapes, that I was hurt, and he wants to help me. Because that's what Marshall does.

"It's for the commissioner," I blurt. "An assignment for my new job."

My words strike him. He sits back and blinks, the chair protesting once more.

"I see. Well, we can't let you disappoint the commissioner, can we?" His question hangs suspended between us in the air. I've just broken whatever it is we had. Our mutual disdain for the town's leader was always something I could count on. But now I've abandoned him for the monster. Copeland doesn't allow security cameras in New Harper. If it were true that he sent me, that implies I told the commissioner about the cameras. I can see the anger brimming in the tight set of Marshall's shoulders, but the deep lines of his face all point to sadness. He's disappointed. In me or in himself, I'm not sure.

"You may use my computer. I need to go check on everyone." He pulls out the drives and shows me how he labeled them by date, then leaves me in the office.

My eyes sting, but there's no time to feel sorry for myself.

One breath. In. Out.

I take a seat behind the desk and examine the drives. There are months of video here. When would Vanessa have come in? I pull out my phone and find Jace's number.

He answers on the first ring. "What happened? Are you okay?"

"Calm down." His urgency is putting me on edge. "I have a quick question. What day did you say Vanessa disappeared?"

"It's been a week now," he answers without hesitation.

One week. Assuming she also found Hazelgrove with blood and water like I did, that would mean she was on her period a week ago. Did she find the green card before I did? Did she solve the same cipher? Or did Hazelgrove appear in her dreams too?

The day I found it was the first time I ever noticed the card on that shelf. But it was replaced after I took it, which means someone must be monitoring it. Watching for when it's taken and leaving another. How though? Only a handful of people know Marshall keeps cameras in the store. We haven't had anyone loitering in the shop.

I'm getting off track.

The date. The pads. Most of the pads from her box were missing when I opened it to borrow one. She could have already used a few boxes, which would mean months of possibilities. But if it were her first box, does that mean she bought it last week?

I sort through drives until I find the one with the correct dates, then plug it into the computer.

"You still there?" Jace's voice cracks through my phone on the desk. I pick it up.

"Yes, I'm here. I'm taking some wild guesses about when she might have come here." I keep the phone to my ear while I scrub through the hours of security camera video. It's a rotating system. Four cameras around the store. Since it's a square layout, the whole shopping floor is at least somewhat visible from each camera. Each gives a better view of its respective side. I skip over the daylight hours and watch the ones at night after it's already dark outside, when it's most likely Vanessa would have snuck out.

"You're looking at the video? Do you see anything?" Jace asks.

"Not yet," I mumble. I hear his soft breath through the speaker while I continue to comb my eyes over the computer screen. I scan up and down each aisle, checking every face. "Wait."

I pause it.

"Do you see Vanessa?"

It takes me a second to answer. "I see Demelza." The red hair is unmistakable. The white dress she wore in Hazelgrove is replaced by jeans and a black jacket. She stands in the aisle where we stock the female products. "Hold on." I let the video play again, keeping a finger ready to stop it. I wait for the camera angle to switch, then pause it again. "There she is." A shorter frame with long dark hair tucked under a baseball cap stands near Demelza. I've seen the same cap on the counter at their cabin. "Jace, it's Vanessa. She was here, and Demelza talked to her."

"When? What happened?"

I let the video play, keeping my eyes on the pair. Their lips move. Vanessa goes to the cashier to check out while Demelza loiters in the aisle. Vanessa exits the store and vanishes into the night. I watch Demelza. She doesn't leave yet. I scrub the video ahead slowly. Demelza talks to three more women in that aisle. Before exiting the store, she pulls something green from her pocket and slips it between the boxes. The card.

"Sariah, what do you see?" Jace urges.

The door to the office swings open, making me jump. I rush to hang up the phone.

"Find what you needed?" Marshall ambles to the desk. I click out of the video and eject the drive.

"I did. Thank you, Marshall. I owe you one." I get up and grab my bag.

He puts his hands on his hips and coughs. "You don't owe me anything, Sar. But if you ever need any help, you tell me." He won't give words to his suspicions, but his generosity invites tears back to my eyes, and my chest burns.

I nod once and duck my head, waving as I head out the back door.

I wipe the stupid tears from my face while I walk, making a beeline out of the parking lot. Jace parked down the street, a few shops away, to avoid attention.

Before I make it far, a black car rolls up just ahead of me on the curb, its tires screeching. Panic shoots into my chest.

I walk faster, hoping I can pass by unnoticed. The back window rolls down, and I can't help glancing to see who's inside. When I do, my feet freeze, locking me in place. From the back of his black sedan, Commissioner Copeland waves me over.

TWENTY

My skin prickles with fear as I slide against the leather seat. The commissioner motions for me to close the door. He waits to speak until the window rolls up.

"Hello, Sariah. I know your shift isn't until tomorrow, but I have a question for you." He looks less charming than usual, more serious, his practiced smile lasting only long enough to complete the greeting. I push my hip as close to my door as I can, beads of sweat forming on my lower spine, my breath shallow. I wait for him to continue.

"You used to see a psychiatrist. A few of them if your records are correct." He still hasn't asked a question, so I wait. "Could you elaborate on why you met with these doctors?" His eyes stay on me in a way they haven't before. Curious. Calculating. Like I'm a puzzle instead of a plaything.

I swallow. "There's not much to explain. I used to have nightmares when I was younger. I outgrew them."

"Hmm. Well, we all have scary dreams now and then." His piercing eyes scan every inch of my body as he shifts to face me, a predator analyzing its prey. "What made it necessary for you to see a doctor about them?"

It takes everything in me to keep from shaking. I'm not sure why he's asking me things that I'm sure Audrey has explained to him. "The dreams seemed very real at the time. My mother wanted to make sure I was okay. It wasn't a big deal." The truth is, Audrey was losing her mind from lack of sleep. I'd either wake up screaming or she'd come to check on me and I wouldn't be in bed. The doctors chalked it up to sleepwalking. As I grew older, I tried harder to control myself so I wouldn't wake her anymore. When she stopped waking, she stopped worrying.

"What about them seemed real? What do you mean by that?" He inches closer. I don't dare break eye contact for fear he'll take it back by force.

"Nothing. I had an overactive imagination." According to most of the doctors, that was my condition verbatim.

"And now, you don't have these vivid dreams?" The question drips with skepticism.

I shake my head in reply.

He takes a long, slow breath through his nose. He's so close now that the exhale stirs the hairs draping over my shoulder. I've seen this hunger in him a hundred times. He wants something. But not me today. No, today he wants information. It makes me wonder if he's involved with Demelza's operation, or if he knows about it at all. My throat is tight. I wouldn't dare bring it up either way.

"You may leave." He waves a dismissive hand as he pulls away. "I'll be seeing you soon. Tell your mother to call tonight. I have questions for her." He's done with me now, staring at the divider between him and his driver.

I don't need any more permission to escape from his car. I pull the handle and jump out as quickly as I can, barely refraining from slamming the door.

TWENTY-ONE

I walk away at full speed and turn a corner to see if Copeland will follow me. His car passes the alley, so I loop around to the spot where Jace should be waiting. Relief trickles through me at the sight of his station wagon, my shoulders finally dropping from my ears.

Jace is pacing at the front of the car, phone tight in one hand, the other tapping the silver hood. His eyes land on me, and his expression softens for a fraction of a second before worry overtakes the set of his features again.

"What happened? I've been calling and texting for the last ten minutes. I thought you were hurt." He's frantically scanning me up and down, checking for a new wound.

"I'm fine. When I left the shop, Copeland drove up. He wanted to talk to me. It was no big deal." It's not a lie. It could have been so much worse. I consider myself lucky this time. And I don't want to dwell on it anymore. I move to open the passenger door, but Jace steps between me and the car.

His expression darkens. "What do mean it's no big deal? You hung up your phone out of nowhere and now you're telling me you were stuck in a car with Copeland? After everything that man has done to you, I'm supposed to believe you're fine?"

My muscles turn rigid. What is he getting at? "What exactly do you know about what Copeland has done to me?" I haven't so much as insinuated the nature of the commissioner's relationship to me. No one else knows.

"I know everything you've told me, Sariah." Jace rubs a hand over his face. "Or that you will tell me, I guess. The point is, I know what he's done. He shouldn't have the opportunity to lay a finger on you ever again. You don't have to put yourself around him. If I'd known he was here, I would have..." He trails off, losing his words, his fists flexing.

The skin of my neck flushes with indignation. My whole life has revolved around keeping this secret, and he waltzes into it one day somehow knowing? My jaw trembles, my stomach twisting into knots. I remember when I caught a glimpse of his room, the sketches covering the wall and his desk. "That's why you didn't want me to take the job. Not because you thought he was responsible for taking your sister, but because you knew how he treats me." The words come out hushed and strangled. I've never told anyone about the commissioner, and I feel like something's been taken from me in Jace's knowing. Like after so much struggle and pain, I've somehow failed. His gaze on me now is like wind on raw flesh. Everything has been stripped away. He can see the ugliest piece of who I am. My throat constricts. I stare at my shoes.

"Sariah, look at me." Jace closes the gap between us, lowering his voice so only I can hear it. He softly lifts my chin with a firm finger. I keep my eyes turned down, blocking him out. "Sariah, please." He breathes. The plea is so sincere.

Slowly, I lift my heavy eyes to meet his.

He places a hand lightly on either side of my face, his fingers brushing the nape of my neck. The touch is fragile. All I can see is him. "You listen to me. No one deserves the life you've been living. You have the right to be safe."

I can't stop the tears that well in my eyes, but I do my best to keep the sob stuffed in my throat. My feet itch to run and hide and never return. Instead, they stick to the ground, my muscles turning to stone.

Jace brushes away a tear from my cheek with his thumb. There's a war in his eyes, then he sucks in a breath and whispers, "I'll stop if you want me to." He wraps his arms around me, pulling me close to his chest. He's warm. His arms don't crush me. They hold me steady. My forehead rubs the worn fabric of his shirt, pine and soap and salt encircling me.

I break. The sob rips from me, and more pour out after it. His chin rests on top of my head, and his hand strokes my hair. There's a ball of panic rattling inside my ribcage, urging me to fight, to flee, to save myself. But the rise and fall of Jace's chest is like a balm to my frayed nerves. He's not hurting me, not forcing me to move a certain way, not taking anything. As the panic eases, the pain and the sadness flood into me. I've held all the hurt back for so long, but the dam has burst. I let my aching arms wrap around his middle, my fingers gripping the fabric of his shirt like a lifeline. We stay that way for a few minutes, then my body sags, all the energy seeping out of me, the sobs still racking my frame. He picks me up and takes me to the back seat of the station wagon. He manages to climb in with me without breaking contact, then closes the door.

"Just to give you more privacy," he whispers into my ear, "you tell me to move, and I will." He adjusts in the seat, nestling me closer, his fingers drawing steady lines up and down my arm. The car should make me panic, alarm bells ring in my skull. But this isn't anything like the other night. No one has ever touched me like this, with gentleness and compassion. My curiosity beats my fear, and I let myself melt against him, my screaming muscles sighing in relief. The tears keep coming, but I focus on his steady breathing and will my breath to sync to his.

One breath. In. Out.

One breath. In. Out.

Over and over again, until I no longer have to think about filling my lungs. Until my mind quiets.

Once the crying is under control, I lean back to look at Jace. Again, he uses his thumb to wipe the water from my cheek, cupping my face in his hand for all of a second before he withdraws it. I'm surprised at the smattering of tears under his blue eyes. He shifts slightly and digs in his pocket before pulling out a piece of fabric and extending it to me.

"What's that?" I croak.

"You can use it to blow your nose." My cheeks redden, and I snatch it from him, turning my whole body away to wipe the snot from my face. I glance back at his shirt. It's completely soaked and wrinkled.

I bury my face in my hands and groan.

He laughs softly and reaches over to unwrap the rag from

my fist, then tosses it to the floor. "We'll wash it back at the cabin."
He traces his fingertips up and down my spine. "Sariah, there's
something I want to tell you," Jace says solemnly.

I peek at him from between my fingers. He's being so kind,
but I am mortified.

"I'm not sure the best way to say this." His other hand comes
to rest on my knee. I'd be lying if I said the contact didn't feel good,
but the panic living in my body wakes again. Did I misread what was
happening here? Is he simply more patient than the other men, but
now he'll tell me what he expects me to do, what he will make me
do?

He looks at me and waits a beat.

"What?" I demand in my raspy voice.

He takes a deep breath. "There's a granola bar in the center
console. I would offer it to you, but I think we're going to need to
split it, because I am so hungry."

I stare at him, incredulous. A smile pulls at his lips, and I
whack him on the arm. "Are you serious?" I glare.

"Oh, gravely serious, yes. I mean, of course, we can get more
food at home, but you know how long the drive is, and I don't think
I can wait that long to eat." He shrugs.

I disentangle myself from him, the anger ebbing away. I
haven't seen him joke before. He looks so... comfortable. "All right
then, let's see this granola bar. If there's no chocolate in it, I might
let you have the whole thing."

"Well, of course there's chocolate. I'm not a maniac." He
scoffs. He opens the door and helps me into the passenger seat.

Once behind the wheel, he opens the middle console and pulls out the wrapped bar. He opens it and breaks it in half, handing me a piece.

I accept it but take his hand, so he'll look at me. "Thank you," I say softly.

The corner of his mouth pulls up again. A quick smile before he takes a bite and turns on the car.

"There actually is one other thing I need to talk to you about." He admits as he pulls onto the road. "I'd like to teach you how to defend yourself."

TWENTY-TWO

MY SOCKED FEET BOUNCE in tiny up and down motions over the rug, my arms wrapped around my middle as I sit on the couch and watch Jace push the other furniture up against the walls of his living room. He turns to face me and claps his hands, rubbing his palms together while gathering his thoughts.

"Okay," he says, "let's get started."

I offer him a small nod. We stare at each other, neither of us sure what to do first.

Jace initiates. "You'll have to stand up." He steps into the middle of the cleared space. I nod again and rise to my feet.

One breath. In. Out.

I step forward so that there are only two paces between our bodies. Being this close to a man would usually send my anxiety soaring, and I'm surprised to find myself filled not with fear, but anticipation.

"Let's just see what you've got, then I can offer some tips. I'll approach and you show me how you would get away." He raises his arms like he'll try to grab me but waits for me to confirm I'm ready.

I widen my stance and dip my chin. He rushes me with more speed than I expected, and I stumble back. My calves hit the couch and my knees collapse, plummeting me back into a sitting position on the couch. The force snaps my head down to my chest, and my back molars snap onto my tongue, slicing into the side of it. The metallic taste of blood fills my mouth. My eyes water from the sudden pain, but the embarrassment that washes over me is far more palpable. I look up sheepishly to where Jace halted his advance.

"You okay?" He asks, his brows drawn together. He drops his arms and approaches, but I wave him off and swallow, resisting the urge to be sick.

"I'm fine. Let's try again." I find my feet again and try to focus.

Jace eyes me warily but relents. "Okay. Well, choosing not to engage is a valid option if you have an opening to run. If the exit is behind you, the obvious choice would be to leave as quickly as possible, without letting Copeland get his hands on you in the first place. So that's a good instinct."

I blush at the compliment. He doesn't bother mentioning the fact that I didn't look where I was going and ended up in a worse position than I started in. "And if the exit isn't an option?" My stomach curdles knowing it won't be.

Jace's mouth forms a grim line. "Then we plan a way for you to incapacitate him long enough to escape."

My heart rate accelerates imagining the commissioner's office, thinking of being stuck there again, with him. The memory alone of the heavy, cloying atmosphere in that space invades all my senses and shoots panic into my chest. I don't want to be his victim again. Never again. I release a shuddering breath. "Show me."

Jace's face remains serious, but the request lights something in his eyes. Excitement? Determination? He backs up and I follow, step for step, resetting to the center of the room.

"Copeland is bigger than you, so you have to be strategic to overpower him. You'll have to use your whole body. You've already shown me you can throw a punch, but now I want you to push me. Try to shove me over." He motions for me to proceed.

"What, just push you over onto the floor?" I shift my weight. I understand the necessity, but I don't want to hurt Jace. Maybe that's giving myself too much credit though. I remember helping Marshall carry Jace when he was unconscious, nearly dropping him because he is so heavy. There's a good chance I can't push him over if I do try.

"Stop overthinking it, Sariah. Just come at me." His stance is strong, but he doesn't move to put up a fight, just waves me towards him.

Okay. I lurch forward, lifting my arms and shoving both hands into his chest. His body moves backwards with the force, but he catches himself easily by stepping one foot back. Then he closes a hand around each of my wrists, trapping me. I pull them away, but he doesn't let go.

"Leading with your hands will make it easier to grab you. You want to keep your hands free." He releases me and changes his stance, stepping one foot back and lowering his front leg into a lunge. "I'll show you how to use your whole body, but it means knocking you to the ground. Are you ready?"

I don't relish the idea of earning new bruises so soon but

consent anyway. "Ready." He goes from standing in front of me to dropping low, leaning his shoulder into my chest, and wrapping his hands around the back of my knees and giving a swift pull. I fall, albeit gently, onto the rug. Then he's on top of me, pinning each of my arms to the ground with his hands, keeping his head and chest high, but locking my hips against the ground with his own. I can tell he's not putting his full weight into the maneuver. He's being gentle with me.

"How was that? Did you follow the whole thing?" He asks from above me.

"Yes, but..." I swallow against the blood still slowly pooling into my mouth.

"What?"

"But Copeland won't be so soft with me. You need to show me how to do it for real."

Jace moves his hands off me, lowering onto his elbows at my sides, and drops a knee between my splayed legs, freeing my hips. This brings his face closer to mine, and I notice the stubble that shades his jaw.

His breath is hot. "If you're ready."

"I think I have to be."

He leans back to regain his footing and takes my hand to pull me with him. Then he retrieves a couple of pillows from the couch by the wall. "I'll go harder, but we're putting these down so you don't whack your head against the floor. The last thing we need is for you to get concussed."

"Ever the physician." I mumble.

"What was that?" he asks while placing the pillows into position.

"Nothing." My cheeks flame again.

He circles back to face me and narrows his eyes, barely concealing a smirk. He sees too much of me, and I'm suddenly self-conscious.

"Well, come on." I snap. He laughs, then bites his lip.

I don't see it coming this time. Instead of distinct segments, he puts me on my back in one fluid motion, and once again he's on top of me. And he was right about the pillow. Without it, my head would definitely have smashed against the ground. The wind is knocked out of me. His grip is tighter around my forearms. His hips press against mine with his full weight. I squirm against him, but he's like stone. I'm really trapped this time.

The panic sets in. I look up at his face, but I don't see Jace. Instead, I see Erebus Copeland, his charming smile replaced by insatiable greed. Behind him looms the dark outline of the ceiling in his office, the sconces on the walls creating orbs of yellow in the corners of my vision. His thick cologne overwhelms my nose, and I choke on the scent. I squeeze my eyes shut to escape from the scene.

"Sariah."

I lay perfectly still, shutting everything out.

"Sariah!" The pressure disappears from my body, and a strong hand shakes my shoulder until my eyes flutter open. Copeland is gone, his office vanished, replaced by the warm lights of the living room and Jace's face above me.

"Are you okay? You froze up."

Slowly, I push back and sit up, wrapping my arms around my shins.

One breath. In. Out.

He's still looking at me, waiting for me to reply.

"I'm fine." It's clear he doesn't believe me from the concern lining his forehead. But what did I expect? I don't believe myself either. "Let's go again."

"Sariah—"

"Let's go again." I cut him off. I stand, and he follows my lead. He opens his mouth to say something, but I go on the offensive, lunging to shove my shoulder against his chest and stooping to pull out his legs. He crashes to the floor and I fall with him, but I've caught him by surprise. I use the extra seconds of confusion to wrestle myself up high enough to pin his arms, though that means my hips press into his stomach. At least I got him down.

Then the world spins. He flips us both over, putting me on my back again, this time with his whole body pressed over mine. But he gets up quickly, sitting back and scooting away.

"You managed to catch me off guard. I'll give you that. But maybe we should give you a break for a minute." He muses. He looks at me with caution, like a bomb he's scared will detonate.

"No. Teach me something else." I refuse to address the freezing. All I want is to learn how to move.

Sweat rolls down the back of my neck. We've been training for over an hour, and I don't feel any more prepared to confront Copeland in the morning. My muscles ache. After everything that has happened these past couple of days, I am so horribly tired. Every bruise on my body begs me to stop and lie down.

Jace sits on the floor and heaves a sigh. "I'm going about this wrong." He stares at the ceiling, and I see the cogs in his mind whir. "You're not going to remember most of these moves, and Copeland is so much bigger than you. It will be impossible for you to overpower him by brute strength." He shakes his head, thinking.

"Thanks for the confidence boost." I mutter. He's right, though. Jace has walked me through a dozen twists, punches, and grabs. But he's taking it slow and gentle, as a teacher, not a real attacker. I know I could fight with everything I have, and it would still take him less than a minute to pin me. My body shuts down when I'm attacked, probably because it knows fighting would be pointless. It's safer to play the rag doll. I can't fight self-preservation.

I swallow back the sour taste in my mouth. "Let's just call it a night. If I'm lucky, there will be some actual work involved at this job. Hopefully, I can use the access to find out more about Demelza."

"About that," Ian walks in from the lab, a laptop balanced in one hand, "I've been doing my best to hack the city's database, and there is no mention of a Demelza anywhere. But I did find something interesting in the schematics of city hall." He sets the computer on the coffee table, and we flock to see the screen. It's a simple black-and-white floor plan, thin lines marking the walls between rooms, each one labeled in tiny print. He points to one room in particular.

"Records room." Jace reads aloud. "As in physical records?" He looks to his brother for confirmation.

Ian nods. "As far as I can tell. My guess is the records kept in that room are ones Copeland doesn't want floating around in any databases. If he keeps information about Demelza in there, then that's what we need to find."

I chew my bottom lip, tucking the location away in my brain. I wish I knew more about what I will be doing tomorrow. This whole plan feels like a shot in the dark. But it's the only shot we have.

"I have an idea." Jace gets to his feet and leaves to the lab. He returns, holding something.

My heart drops to my feet when I see it. I cut in before he has a chance to say a word. "No." I'm up and walking backward, putting distance between myself and it.

He stops, stunned. "Just let me explain—"

"I won't use it." My stare locks on the blade in his hand, small and black, with two sharp edges that meet in a wicked point.

"It could be your best option, Sariah. It's ceramic, so it won't set off the metal detectors, and at close range you've got the element of surprise on your side. It would only take a quick jab or two, and Copeland would back off enough for you to run." He holds the knife out to me. I process his logic, but all I can do is shake my head.

"I won't use a knife. Anything else, but I won't use that." I spit the last word at the weapon.

Ian glances between us, eyebrows high on his forehead. "You could always use a pen." He offers.

Jace watches me a moment longer, then bites his cheek and stalks away, this time to his room. When he reemerges, he holds out an onyx-hued stick. "Here." He's frustrated, but he keeps his tone even.

I take it and run my fingers over the smooth cold surface.

"Open it." He instructs, arms folded over his chest.

I remove the heavy cap, and the pointed end of the fountain pen winks at me under the fluorescent lights. Under normal circumstances it would seem innocuous, but after seeing the knife, the metal tip feels lethal.

"So, what exactly do you expect me to do with this?" I swallow again.

Jace comes closer, his voice low. "I can't be in there with you tomorrow. It would ruin your chances. But I need to know you're safe. If Copeland tries to lay a finger on you, you open this pen and you stab the end wherever you can reach. Wherever it will hurt. Go for soft tissue if you can. Then you run. I'll wait nearby. I'll come and get you. You just have to call me. No matter what, you keep your phone and this pen on your person at all times. Promise me you'll do that. Please?" I'm shocked once again at the way he stares straight into me. The way he seems to know me down to my core.

Ever since the incident in the car, he's been opening up, letting me see him. And he's dead set on trying to keep me as safe as he can without jeopardizing our plan. It's getting harder not to trust him. To keep my own guard up.

"Okay. I promise."

TWENTY-THREE

THE CEMENT STAIRS LEADING up to the gray government office building are taller than necessary. I push my knees that extra few inches higher to climb them, a burn starting in the muscles of my legs. The steep angle makes the commissioner seem even more menacing than usual.

Of course, no one else seems to notice.

They all greet him with large smiles and handshakes, craving his approval and acknowledgement. He gives it, but in a way that leaves them feeling like they've disappointed him. They walk on, wondering what else they can do to please him. I can read the look on their faces because it is one I wore often as a child.

I clear the final step, Copeland waiting for me with a close-lipped smile.

One breath. In. Out.

He greets me with more enthusiasm than the others. "Sariah, how lovely it is to see you here. I am so glad you chose to join me at last. I have meetings to attend to, but this," he wraps an arm around my shoulders and pivots me toward another woman who I recognize from the store, "is Layla. She is my assistant, and she will help you settle in." His hand squeezes my upper arm, his thumb stroking, the rest of him pressed up against my other side. "I'll leave you ladies to it." He walks behind me toward the front doors, leaving me chilled.

"Hello," Layla starts, extending her hand to shake mine. Firm. She's sure of herself, but I see a twinge of sympathy in her smile. "Follow me. I'll help you get your paperwork sorted and show you around." She leads me through large iron-framed doors, then under the metal detectors. The detectors beep as I pass, and a guard blocks my path.

"Step to this table and empty your pockets and purse. Move slowly." He's got a baton in hand, and a blade sheathed at his belt. My hands shake a bit, but I do as he says. I didn't bring much, just a few basics in my purse that he seems mildly bored by. Then I pull my phone and the fountain pen from my front pockets and set them on the table. The pen lands with an audible click. The guard secures the baton back onto his belt and reaches for the pen. He opens the cap and inspects it, then closes it and puts it back down. "All clear. Move along."

Layla waits a few paces off.

I hurry to gather my belongings so we can continue.

We pass the reception area and pass through an ornate doorway at the back of the cavernous space. It's marked with a white sign that reads: Employees Only.

"Stand here, please. I'm going to get your picture for your name card." I stand on the taped X on the floor, and she clicks a button on a camera. She places the camera on a pad next to a computer and taps a few keys.

"Perfect. That will print right over here." She walks to a gray machine in the corner that spits out a silver plastic card, which she attaches to my collar with a small metal clasp. My wide-eyed face stares at me above my embossed name. "Don't lose this. It serves as identification and your key card to get into the building and into any rooms you'll need to access."

I nod once. "So, what will I do as an intern? The commissioner didn't tell me any specifics."

"Oh, this and that." She moves things around on a table, then huffs and turns to face me. "To tell you the truth, I was disappointed when I heard you were joining us. Not because of you. You seem lovely. But I'm no stranger to how the commissioner operates, and he seemed extra happy about having you here. He wasn't lying. The pay is good. But if there's nothing else he's holding over you, you should tell him you've changed your mind. Get out as soon as possible. I'll show you around today, so he won't be suspicious. But after that, you can tell him it wasn't what you were expecting."

For a moment, I can't speak. Layla is being so forward. Her insinuations make me both hate and fear the commissioner more than before. He's likely got the whole staff wrapped around his finger.

"I — I can't go," I say. "I need to be here."

Layla frowns. "Well, I guess we have something in common. Let's get started then. I'll give you the tour and then show you where you'll be spending most of your time."

The office building is immense. Full of overlapping hallways, marble floors, and absurdly high ceilings. Layla assures me I won't need to remember where everything is. The interns usually stay in a certain section of the building. When she brings me to an office with a large wooden desk, she nods to another door directly across from it. "That's the commissioner's office. You'll be reporting to me, and I report to him. You're one of five employees we've got in this rotation, and he takes weekends off, so you're scheduled for one day a week." She skirts the desk and opens a drawer to retrieve a file. "Come sit." She pulls out the chair at the desk for me. "This is your contract. I need you to sign this so I can get it into the system."

I scan the contents of the contract, stopping cold when I see the pay rate. "I only come in one day a week, and I'm paid this much? That has to be a mistake."

Layla's frown returns. "The commissioner feels his interns perform best when they have had adequate rest. He likes everyone to be... fresh." The way she's looking at me reiterates her warning from before.

My skin crawls, but I knew what I was getting into when I placed the phone call. The sooner I find the information Jace and Ian need, the sooner I can disappear.

"You said this is his office, right?" I rise and walk to the door. Next to it on the wall, I notice a sleek silver rectangle. Layla has been using similar ones all day to unlock doors with her keycard. I hold mine up to it, but nothing happens.

"It is, and you won't have access to enter it yourself. He'll retrieve you if he needs you. Your key can unlock the main building, this room, and a handful of others. The kitchen, the assembly hall, the records room, and the press room."

My ears perk at the mention of the records room, but I try not to reveal anything in my expression.

"Sariah, listen to me." Layla comes closer, her voice a whisper now. "The commissioner is powerful, and he has the means to obtain anything he wants. Whatever he is baiting you with, I am sorry you feel you must do this. Please know I will do my very best to mitigate your contact with him." Tears shine at the rims of her eyes.

A shiver of fear slithers down my back.

"Just give it some thought." She sniffs and straightens. "Let's take that tour." A pasted smile overtakes her face. She's quick on her stilettos and is in the hall before I can stand to follow. I pat the pen in my pocket.

One breath. In. Out.

When I catch up with her in the hallway, words spew over her shoulder, her brisk steps clacking against the tile. "We'll start in the records room. You may be sent here to retrieve a file on occasion. All the information is confidential, so it is essential that you read only the label name. If you're caught opening files or tampering with them in any way, the commissioner will take disciplinary action." She gives me a hard look. "Don't get caught reading a file."

The warning accompanies a sudden stop in front of a windowless metal door. The silver pad next to it gleams, and a sinking sensation fills my gut. Reaching the records room this early into the job is fortunate. Too good to be true, really. A set up?

"Try your key." Layla motions for me to put my card on the pad. When I do, a solid click sounds within the door.

Inside, a twelve-by-twelve foot white room sits silent.

The thick gray carpet absorbs the movement of our feet. Sentinels in the form of khaki filing cabinets line the outer walls of the space, and four neat rows in the middle of the floor. The overhead lights shine bright, and I note the space is windowless, with only the one door. It smells like old paper.

Layla carries on while I orient myself. "We label everything here alphabetically by last name." She points at the stickers on the cabinets that mark which letter it contains.

Last name. I don't know Demelza's last name.

It will take forever to check every file.

A buzzing erupts in Layla's pocket. She pulls out her phone and puts it to her ear.

"Yes? She's here. I understand. I just thought we could finish the tour." Her lips press into a flat line. "Yes, sir. I will bring her right away." She sighs in defeat as she slips away the phone.

An apology takes shape in the draw of her eyebrows and the tilt of her lips.

"Commissioner Copeland has requested to see you now."

TWENTY-FOUR

"MY DEAR, SARIAH. IT has been too long since I've enjoyed your company here." Erebus Copeland leans comfortably in his high-backed chair, sharp leather shoes propped up on his desk. The curiosity and seriousness from his car are gone. His signature smile is back on his face, a reminder that I'm the prey.

I haven't set foot in this office in years. I've done every possible thing to avoid it. But now I'm here, the choking scent of his cologne and heavy dark wood fill the space, pressing the memories down on my chest until I struggle to fill my lungs with air. Layla closes the door behind me, and I hear a mechanical whirring, followed by the weighted click of the lock.

He still keeps it there. Right on the front corner of his desk in its black marble stand.

His favorite knife.

He always gave me a memento after our time together. A reminder of my promise, my end of the bargain. They morphed from gifts and trinkets into something else the older I got.

I tear my eyes from the blade.

Why did I agree to come here? I've screwed everything up. I should have just kept working at Marshall's and kept my head down.

For all I know, Copeland might not have any information regarding Demelza.

"Take a seat." He gestures to one of the chairs facing his desk.

I want to run.

I slide my hand into my pocket and feel the cold touch of the pen. My index finger runs over the lip of the cap. It would only require an ounce of pressure to pop it off and expose the sharp end. I'd have time to pull it out if he stood up to move closer.

My chest burns, and I realize I've neglected to draw a breath since crossing the threshold onto the dark red carpet.

Slowly and silently, I inhale through my nose and take measured steps forward. I force my knees to bend, sitting across the massive expanse of desk that leaves him entirely too close to me. My hands slide over the wooden scrolls of the armrests carved into my chair. My finger travels the ridge of the swirl, and with that small movement I'm twelve years old again. Old enough to know not to cry in this room. To know what happens here. And to know the only power I hold is to keep it a secret. If I can keep it a secret, my mother won't have to suffer. That's what he promises me. If I can't escape the hurt, the least I can do is spare her.

"Sariah, I must admit I'm curious, what finally changed your mind?" Copeland drops his feet to the floor so he can lean forward, yanking me from my thoughts.

"Changed my mind?"

"About working here."

I have to get it together. I'm here for a reason.

One breath. In. Out.

Play the game.

If I play it right, I'll never have to come here again.

I can't tell him about Jace and Ian. Or the dreams. I wonder if I can get him to tell me something about Demelza? Which cards can I safely play? Which pieces on the board can I sacrifice?

How long can I keep him talking before the inevitable comes for me?

"I thought it would be a good opportunity to learn more about New Harper."

How much will he read into that?

"In what way?" His face is impenetrable.

"The history. How it got started." It might be too much, questioning the origin of the town. It never once crossed my mind before Ian brought the subject to my attention.

"You've been talking with your mother, I take it?" He leans back, eyes never straying from my face.

I hope I keep it composed as I take in his question. I know Audrey has worked with him for a long time. Does he mean she's been around since the founding of the town? I weigh my response. "She won't say much about it. That's why I'm here."

He nods twice. "And you know why I've invited you here." He scoots his chair back from his desk and spreads his legs wide. I calculated wrong. He's done talking.

My hand slides to the pen in my pocket. Sweat breaks out along my spine.

"To intern." Even I can hear how hopeless the words sound falling from my lips.

He smiles again. "Let's make this like old times."

I envision the wicked tip of the fountain pen digging into his neck, right at the base of his jaw. His eyes wide with surprise, his strangled, angry cry filling the room as the blood erupts from his throat.

But I wouldn't see the blood. I would already be running.

Two doors between me and the hallway. Another two to exit the building. Then I run straight to Jace's car down the road. He'll peel out. We'll drive into the woods. This will be over. We'll find another way. I'll talk sense into Vanessa. I'll do something, anything else.

Copeland stands and comes around the heavy desk. He leans against it right in front of me. I press the lid off the pen with the pad of my thumb. The fabric muffles the pop. His fingers reach out to tuck my hair behind my ear, then crawl their way around the back of my head to secure my skull in his grip.

My whole body turns to stone. My fingers turn to ice against the pen.

I can't do it.

I can't stop this.

TWENTY-FIVE

M Y SHAKY FINGERS STRUGGLE to button my blouse when the knocks strike the door. The commissioner invites Layla into the office. She won't look in my direction.

I smooth down the fabric of my clothes, making sure everything is in place.

One breath.

One breath.

It won't come.

My chest heaves in micro-movements. My body will only give me enough oxygen to survive the torture. It wants to shut down, to give up, to be done. I do too.

Their voices float around me. I hear them, but like I'm under water. A world away but somehow standing in the same room. Everything is garbled and too heavy and only half there.

At some point, my name breaks through.

"Sariah." Layla speaks. "You can come with me. Commissioner, Kedron is expecting your call in two minutes."

If Copeland offers a farewell, I don't notice. I keep my head tucked down, focus on moving my feet.

No one deserves the life you've been living. Jace's voice echoes in my mind. I hold the words, skimming over them again and again. Something brims in my chest, a new sensation. Hot. Painful.

Anger.

But it's more than that.

"I'm so sorry, Sariah. I really didn't expect him to move so fast. I thought I could give you more time." When I look up at her, I realize we've stopped in the records room again. Layla paces the carpeted floor.

"What are we doing in here?" I ask.

She stops, facing me. "It's the quietest room we have. No one can hear you from the hall, and only select employees have access. I thought you might need a minute. To compose yourself."

I hate the look in her eyes. The sympathy. The pity.

"What are you doing here? Why do you work for him?" If she feels so bad for me, why would she keep working this horrible job, sending girl after girl in for Copeland to ruin?

She sniffs. "You're not the only one Erebus has under his thumb. I used to think he really cared about me, you know? That this would be an amazing opportunity to advance my career. I don't think anyone is immune to his charms, but it's harder to look at him the same when you've seen behind the curtain. None of that matters, though. I'm in your same boat. I have to be here. I have my reasons." She steps forward to take my hands in hers. "Sariah, if there is anything I can do for you, any favor, you name it."

I cringe slightly at her touch. My eyes dart away, landing on a filing cabinet.

It takes only seconds for the pieces to click into place like the mechanisms in a lock. If I can set it in motion now, this plan might work.

I look Layla in the eye. "Thank you. I'll keep that in mind." I pat her hands so that I can slip mine away without seeming rude. "Actually, I do have a question. You may not even be able to answer it, but I'd appreciate if you didn't pass it on to the commissioner."

"Of course," she nods. "What is it?"

One breath. In. Out.

I have to take this chance.

"Do you know if there are any records here about a woman named Demelza?"

I watch the flicker of recognition on her face.

"Yes. There was a woman who worked here. A long time ago now. Demelza Hamill?" She searches for confirmation, so I nod.

Hamill. It could be her. At the very least, it gives me somewhere to look.

I hurry to change the subject before she asks any follow-up questions. "So do we need to finish the tour, or have I completed my tasks for the day?" I edge the words with just a tinge of bitterness. The pity returns to her eyes.

"You can go home. I'll see you next week." She turns to open the door. I quickly pull the black pen from my pocket and, when she's not looking, toss it behind a row of cabinets while I cough into my other fist. It lands softly on the padded floor. I exit the room after Layla.

"You met us out front today, right? Did you walk here, or did you drive?" She asks.

"Why?" Has Audrey said anything yet, or do they assume I've still been living at home?

Layla bats her hand in the air. "Oh, it's just that you don't need to park on the street. We've got a parking garage around back with security. You can show them your badge next time."

I tuck that piece of information away for later. "Thank you."

She escorts me to the front doors. "Hold on a second." From her jacket pocket, she slips out a white card and hands it to me. "My direct number is on there. In case you need to call me for anything. I'm serious about that favor." She offers me a sad smile goodbye.

I force my mouth to return it.

TWENTY-SIX

JACE'S EXPRESSION IS GUARDED, his mouth a hard line. I don't answer his barrage of questions until I'm in the passenger seat and we're almost to the edge of town.

"Please, Sariah, talk to me." He's sat through my silence with patience, but the furrow in his brow grows deeper.

"I don't want to talk about Copeland." I force the words out, steeling myself. If I intend to survive this, if this plan is going to succeed, my walls must stay up. No more emotions. I need to keep my head down and focus. And I need Jace and Ian to help me. At least until I have more information.

"I don't want to talk about Copeland." I repeat, firmer. "But I have a plan. There's a chance we can get Demelza's file. If it is hers, we can use whatever is inside to figure out the best way to approach your sister. We have to move fast — we're running out of time."

A million questions burn in Jace's eyes. He looks back at the road so he can pull into the trees. "Running out of time for what?" He voices.

"At best, my bleed will last three more days. That's if we're lucky. Once it's over, we'll have to wait another month before I can revisit Hazelgrove."

His knuckles go white on the steering wheel. "We can't leave her there for a month."

He parks and we walk back to the cabin. Jace is quiet now, thoughts festering.

"This plan of yours — what does it entail?" He opens the door for me. I enter, taking a slow breath.

"A favor. Sneaking around. Maybe some computer system hacking. And I'll need your car."

"Oh, is that all?" He stares me down. The stubble on his jaw has grown darker, only intensifying his weary appearance. Another month of this could very well kill him. I look away.

Walls up.

I step into the elevator, but before I press the button at the top of the wall, Jace reaches up to grab my hand.

"Sariah." He whispers, standing close to me. "Did you use the pen?"

I steal my hand back and swivel my head to look up at him. His pupils are pits of despair. He can already tell what happened. I'm sure of it. I lower my face, allowing my hair to fall like a curtain between us. His body heat radiates over me in the small space. I wrap my arms around my middle, swallowing against the tension in my throat. The soft scent of pine needles and soap wafts off him. I hate how much I've started to like the smell. He's a statue, waiting.

"Not the way you wanted me to." With that, I turn and hit the button. I thought he'd step back, but as the box shutters into motion, he stumbles forward, catching himself against the wall behind my head.

"What can I do?" The words drop into my ear, leaden with sadness, with helplessness. He didn't ask if I'm okay. Maybe he realizes what a stupid question that would be. He doesn't berate me for failing to defend myself. Part of me thought he would.

Because I did.

I failed.

You can help me disappear.

"You can help me find your sister." I say instead. When the door whooshes open, I step out and withdraw to the couch. No more dwelling on Copeland. We're going to sit and talk through my plan. No time to lose.

"Ian, get in here." Jace calls out, anger lacing his tone.

A bleary-eyed Ian appears from the lab, his dark hair stuck up in places.

"You look awful." Jace says. He sits next to me on the couch. I resist the urge to scoot farther away. Then I resist the urge to move closer to him.

Get it together, Sariah.

I settle for straightening my spine and rolling my shoulders back.

Both his hands clench into fists.

"I'm going to walk you through this, and then you're both going to tell me if I'm crazy." Both men wait for me to continue. "I left the pen in the records room. Copeland's assistant offered me a favor, and I'm going to take her up on it tonight. I will inform her that I believe I dropped my pen in there, that it's important to me, and that I want to go find it. She believes I'm in distress right now, so she'll probably honor the request even though it seems silly." At that, Ian narrows his eyes, looking between Jace and me, but doesn't voice his question, so I carry on. "I have my own key card now. I don't know if she'll permit me in the room alone, but if you can duplicate the card, one of you can sneak in after me. Hopefully, she'll just let me go in on my own, but the backup would improve our odds. I have a last name for Demelza. Hamill. We're looking for Demelza Hamill. The records are set up alphabetically by surname. I don't know for certain it's the same woman who took your sister, but it's our only lead. We'll need the car too. We can get out a lot faster if we park in the employee garage. It's risky, but I think speed is our best option. Get in, get the file, get out. We can regroup here and read it. Make a plan. With any luck, I can get to Hazelgrove late tonight and talk to Vanessa. I need time to convince her before my bleed ends." That's only part of what I hope to accomplish in Hazelgrove, but I don't mention more. Their help is crucial. I hyperventilate, not accustomed to talking so much.

A twinge of pain makes me look down at my hands in my lap. I've ripped the skin on my finger open again. Lovely. I wrap the hem of my blouse around it to staunch the blood. Note to self: do not get that finger wet.

"I'll go in with you." Ian pipes up.

"No, Ian, it's not safe. I can't let you." Jace shakes his head, sending an arm along the back of the couch. If I leaned back, it would be around my shoulders. I don't lean back.

Ian is ready to protest, but I cut in. "Hopefully, neither of you will have to follow me. I'll try to get the file myself, but either way it's a moot point unless you can copy this card." I pull the silver rectangle from my pocket and wave it in the air.

Ian snatches it from me and bolts to the lab.

Jace exhales slowly through his nose, running a hand through his hair. "This is a dangerous play, Sariah."

I nod.

"But you're not crazy. I think you've just given us the chance we need to save Vanessa." Gratitude fills his words.

I can't help the guilt that creeps into my chest.

TWENTY-SEVEN

MY THUMB TREMBLES OVER the black keypad. Layla's card sits on the coffee table in front of me, phone number clearly printed in matte ink.

The longer we wait for the cloning process of the keycard to finish, the more doubt stalls my resolve. I could bail on the whole idea. No one will blink twice at a lost pen. I could leave it there.

But where does that leave us? No closer to learning more information about Demelza and Hazelgrove. No closer to escaping from Copeland.

Escape.

That single word causes my eyes to sting. There is no choice really. This plan is my shot, and I'm going to take it.

"Finished!" Ian calls from the lab. He bounds into the living room brandishing two small cards. One silver, one white. "We don't have the exact card, but it should do the job." He hands my silver one back to me before sliding the white one into his pocket.

"Think again, Ian." Jace appears behind me and holds out his hand. His brother begrudgingly pulls the card back out and places it in the outstretched palm. "Come and eat." Jace walks back to the kitchen, and Ian follows. I turn and over the back of the couch

I see Jace set a steaming dish onto the dining table. I've been so in my head that I didn't even hear him cooking. Now that he's brought my attention to the food, my stomach curls inward, the hearty scent of chicken and herbs floating over from the next room. When was the last time I stopped to eat?

Ian is already taking his place when I stand up, inching my way towards the source of the delicious smell. Jace returns to the table with a stack of plates, forks, and knives. He sets them down and slides a chair out, gesturing for me to sit. I widen my gait, heat rushing to my cheeks as I lower myself into the spot. Jace settles into the seat next to mine.

Audrey and I never used the dining table while I was growing up. We grabbed food when we were hungry. A donut from the box she brought home after a shift. Cereal eaten hunched over the kitchen sink. All assortments of packaged snacks from Marshall's store. Sitting here with proper dishes, the smooth wood of the tabletop under my fingertips, feels foreign. Intimate.

Metal clanks against porcelain. When I don't move, Jace trades his full plate for my empty one. Steam fills my nose, and I nearly moan with longing.

"Everything okay?" Jace asks. He and Ian have already started taking bites.

"Fine." I pick up the cold steel of my fork and pierce the prongs into a piece of the meal. When the tender white flesh meets my tongue, my eyelids flutter closed, relief fills my whole being.

After stuffing a few more bites into my mouth, I set the fork down and stop to breathe.

"I didn't know you were such a talented cook."

Jace's loaded fork halts halfway to his mouth, jaw slack. His smile is quick to follow. "My dad taught me. He thought it was an important skill. Especially with the chickens out back."

"Do you have a big freezer outside or something?" I guess it would make sense to keep a lot of food out here.

Ian laughs. "Why don't you go take a look?"

Jace chews and swallows. "Would you like to?"

"What, see a freezer?" I eye my plate, not wanting to part with the amazing meal.

"We haven't shown you outside yet. Come on, we can finish eating after." He wipes his mouth with a napkin and stands.

I follow reluctantly.

We walk through the living room into the lab. At the far end stands a large metal door. He turns a dial on the wall, and I hear a lock disengage. Jace pries the door ajar, and proceeds into the shadowy nothingness beyond.

The muscles around my lower spine clench. I stop before the doorway, squinting into the darkness. How much do I trust Jace? He has no reason to hurt me. Not that others had a reason in the past. Still, he needs my help, which means until Vanessa is home, I'm safe here. That's what I'm counting on, at least.

A whoosh of air lifts strands of hair from my face. Purple light filters down from an opening above, illuminating a dirt staircase.

Jace's figure fills the doorframe at the top of the stairs. "You coming?"

I toe the bottom step, hesitating. Then I climb.

By the time I reach the top, my breath is embarrassingly staggered. But the scene laid before me steals it away altogether.

The setting sun lights the trees that tower around a clearing of grass and wildflowers, bushes interspersed within the tree line. Red berries hang plump on green tendrils close to the dirt. A stream murmurs steadily, sparkling against the shadows between branches. What strikes me most is the quiet. There is nothing besides the natural sounds of the water and the breeze. It's the same tranquility that draws me out to the woods to hike any chance I get. I didn't realize how desperately I needed it now. My shoulders fall half an inch, and I draw a full, deep breath.

Jace reaches into a sack slumped against the side of the cabin. He turns and flings his arm, a spray of small pieces littering the grass. The leaves all around the clearing rustle, and flapping wings fill the space. A flock of chickens eats the seeds.

"So, not a freezer then." A laugh escapes me. This is too absurd. No one other than the farmers keeps live animals in New Harper. I shouldn't be surprised, though. Of course, this is a more practical food supply. One that can reproduce. "What did you say your parents did when they worked for Copeland?"

"They're scientists. They worked on a lot of different projects to help develop the town." Jace crouches down, running the back of his hand over a chicken's feathers. "I wish I'd asked more questions, tried to learn more before they disappeared."

Hadn't Layla said something about Demelza working for Copeland too. I should have asked what her role was. Could she have known Jace's parents? If she did, why would she take their daughter? I'm reaching though. I need the file. Concrete data. Wild guesses will only distract me at this stage.

Still, it would be an intriguing connection.

If Demelza could escape to her own world, could their parents accomplish the same? Which begs yet another question: could I?

A beak comes down on my shoe and jolts me from my thoughts. The chicken pecks around my foot at something in the grass. I step around it, uncertain of the correct way to interact with a live bird.

I move to the tree line, getting a better view of the water. Something about it calls to me, like an invisible rope tied around my middle, reeling me in slowly. Where could it send me if I knew how to control the connection?

Movement in my periphery makes me jump.

Jace. It's only Jace.

One breath. In. Out.

"I can't send you in there alone again." Jace says. He leans against a tall trunk, the golden rays of the sinking sun finding him from spaces between the leaves above, covering him in a patchwork of light and shadow.

A breeze bounces off the water towards us, chilling my arms through the thin sleeves of my top. I didn't think to grab a jacket. He must see me shiver, because he shrugs out of his sweater, pulling it over his head and coming forward to offer it to me. I should decline. I need to avoid all this closeness.

But I don't say anything, instead staring at the knit fibers until my teeth begin chattering. Jace huffs a small laugh and brings the garment over my head himself, pulling it down around my torso. My arms are trapped inside for a moment, but the warmth overrides my nerves. I slide my arms into the sleeves. They're too long, the cuffs falling a few inches past my fingertips, but I curl my fists, squeezing the thick yarn.

It shouldn't feel so good wearing something of his. I don't like the way it puts me at ease. His scent is all-encompassing now, and when I lift my eyes, I find his staring back at me, trailing the lines of my face. His fingers are still tucked around the bottom hem of the sweater, knuckles resting gently against my hips.

"What are you thinking?" I ask quietly.

His chest rises and falls. "That you're so much more beautiful in person than in my dreams."

A fluttering blooms inside me. Fight it, Sariah.

"I know it sounds strange," he continues, "but I've traced your face on paper so many times, trying to get it right. Trying to remember in the moments after I wake up. Holding on to every piece of you I can. Always hoping. I don't know if I ever believed you'd really be here. My family has been isolated in these woods my whole life. I didn't anticipate that changing. And while I wish it were under better circumstances, I can't help how happy I am that you're here. You've given me hope, Sariah. Maybe it's not fair for me to put that on you, but it's true."

"Hope for what, exactly?" The words barely push past my mouth. My whole body is still, caught on his every word, held in place by the intensity of his gaze.

His lips press together. "For a new life. With you. I know I shouldn't say this, especially since you only met me a few days ago, but what I want more than anything is to start somewhere new. To get out of this corrupt town. And I want to do it together. I never really thought it was possible, but you've shown me that it might be." He pauses. "What about you? Obviously, I'm so grateful that you're willing to help us find Vanessa, but after she comes home, what do you think you'll do?"

I'd never considered he might want to leave his family and his home. That the sketches on his wall might indicate a desire for something beyond a temporary favor.

I'd never considered that when I do run away, I might not have to do it alone.

But he's right about one thing. We just met. I still don't know how much of what he's telling me is true. A charming smile and piercing eyes are great tools for a liar.

Still, there is something different about him. I'm all too familiar with the feel of greed in a man's touch. There is none of it in the way Jace holds me now. I'm not even sure he can tell that he's been moving ever closer, bringing our bodies only a finger's length from each other. He's still waiting for my answer.

"Getting out of here sounds pretty good."

He eyes my mouth. Again, it doesn't seem calculated. When he leans in, the movement is fluid, like he's done it a hundred times before, and his neck knows just the way to bend so that our lips can meet. Before they can, I pivot my head, sucking in an audible breath.

The sound snaps him out of whatever trance we were sharing. He removes his fingers from the sweater and takes two quick steps backward.

"Sariah, I'm so sorry." Jace rakes his hands through his hair. "That was stupid. I know I need to give you your space." He mumbles something under his breath.

My eyes sting. I quickly blink the threat of tears into submission. "Jace." I say his name softly.

He stops cursing himself and looks at me.

"You don't have to be sorry." I shrug. "You stopped."

TWENTY-EIGHT

"TELL ME THIS IS going to work." The station wagon's steering wheel grows damp under my palms. I didn't think this through. I've been so desperate, so flustered, that I got sloppy. I overlooked details. "Copeland knows my mom and I only have one car. What if people start asking questions?" Stupid, stupid, stupid. What was I thinking?

"If anyone asks, you tell them with the new job you thought it made sense to get one for yourself. You got a great deal on a used car. No one will bat an eye. Park somewhere shadowed so I can sneak out when it's time," Ian replies from the floor of the backseat. He's only slightly muffled by the blankets we threw back there. They'll keep him hidden in case anyone tries to look in the windows.

"We've been over this, Ian. You're not going in. You're too young to be working there. People will get suspicious." Jace lies scrunched up on the backseat wearing slacks, a blue button-down shirt, and a navy tie. He pushes a pair of brown glasses into place on his nose. Ian groans but doesn't argue.

I called Layla an hour ago and told her about the pen. She said she was still in the office, and that I could come right away. Everything went so fast after that. Jace and Ian became a whirlwind,

running around the house changing clothes and yelling out instructions.

I mostly sat on the couch trying to steel myself. Not that it
did much good. The closer we get to the office, the more my brain
picks apart all the flaws in our hurried plan.

"And you really think you'll be able to slip in doors behind
people? That no one is going to request your identification?" My
shoulders skim my ears. My throat is too dry to swallow.

"I've managed to live in this town without living *in* this
town my entire life. I can handle one building." Jace's voice is so
steady I almost believe him. But he doesn't know the commissioner
like I do. If he's caught — well, I don't want to think about it.

"You guys just need to be quick. In and out. I'll be a lookout,
and I'll let you know when it's safe to return to the car." I didn't like
the idea of bringing Ian, but now that we have actions available to
help his sister, he refuses to waste more time. Or to wait at the cabin.
I hear a few taps from his spot behind my seat. "Earpieces working?"
He whispers.

His voice is double, coming from the car and the little piece
of plastic tucked in my ear. "It's working."

"Mmhm." Jace confirms.

I pull into the parking garage behind the office building. It's
dark now, the sky a gloomy shade of navy. The guard booth is lit
from inside so I can see that it is empty, but a scanner waits in front
of the retractable beam blocking the entrance. I slip my silver card
from my blazer pocket and tap it against the sensor. The beam lifts,
swooshing through the evening air. I roll the window back up to

block out the chill. My teeth grate across my lip as I find a spot in the corner, farther from the overhead lights, and disengage the key from the ignition.

"Repeat the plan for me one more time," Ian prods.

I take a shaky breath. "I go in and walk straight to the records room. If I run into Layla, I'll thank her for letting me come in and tell her I can handle finding the pen. If anyone else asks, I just tell them I'm picking something up. No long conversations."

Jace chimes in. "I'll find my way inside in the next seven minutes and wait outside the records room. You'll send me a message when it's safe to go in. If we're interrupted before we find the file, you'll try to distract whoever it is, and I'll keep searching. Once we find it, we take turns coming back to the car. You'll go first, and I'll follow quickly. I'll meet you down the street if there's a guard in the garage."

"I'll alert you if there's a guard, or anyone else out here." Ian pipes up.

"And if we find nothing after a thorough sweep, we come back to the car and leave." My chest clenches at the thought of leaving empty-handed. I do not possess the nerve to attempt this more than once.

They both reluctantly agree.

"And if I get caught?" This is the part I hate most.

"And if you get caught, we drive to Marshall's and wait for your signal." Ian recites the piece of the plan I made them agree to. It's what I want to hear, but so far Jace won't commit to it.

"Hey, Sariah?" He whispers.

"Hmm?"

"Don't get caught."

I turn to look around the seat at Jace. His gaze bores into mine. He nods once.

I nod back. We can do this. What other choice do we have?

TWENTY-NINE

I OPEN MY DOOR, passing the keys back to Ian just in case. No more thinking. Move. I duck my head as I walk through the door to the building, avoiding eye contact with anyone. It's early evening now, and most people have already gone home. Thankfully, the few employees still milling through the halls look exhausted and ignore me as I pass.

My shoes tap against the hard marble floor, echoing through the quiet hall with its too-high ceiling hanging over me like a guillotine waiting to drop. When I reach the door to the records room, my muscles go rigid.

The chilling touch of eyes caresses my spine, and I turn my head slowly to peer behind me. No one.

I try to shake the feelings off. Stick to the plan.

One breath. In. Out.

I scan my card on the plate beside the door. The thud of the deadbolt disengaging is terrifying against the quiet. My fingers wrap around the cold metal knob, pulling it down, each millisecond stretching into an eternity. Sweat forms at the nape of my neck, my hair trapping the heat.

I pull the door open and scan the space with my eyes.

The room is empty.

Quickly, I close the door behind me, leaving it just slightly ajar, so that the lock hangs apart from the frame. I pull my phone from my pocket to send the two-letter message.

I move toward the metal cabinets, trying to decide the best way to start this search when muffled staccato footsteps click from the hallway. Jace couldn't have been that fast. Besides, it sounds like stilettos.

My face is hot, palms clammy.

The door swings open and Layla enters, deftly balancing a mountain of color-coded folders on one arm, her eyebrows pulled together in confusion.

"Oh!" She jumps when she sees me, nearly toppling the files. "It's you, Sariah. You startled me." She laughs, placing a hand over her heart. "Did you find what you needed?" She uses her foot to push the door fully closed.

I eye the lock as it turns, my stomach sinking.

"Sariah?"

"Oh. Yes. I mean, I was about to look." I hurry over to the cabinet I dropped the pen behind earlier. It's still there, lying cockeyed on the carpet. I stoop to pick it up and brandish it so that she can see. "So silly of me to drop it. Thanks for letting me come in to grab it."

I linger in my spot. What am I supposed to do now? I can't just poke around while she's in here working.

"Not a problem." She smiles sheepishly. "Actually, while you're here, would you mind grabbing a few of these?" Layla steps toward me, unsteady under the weight. I put out my hands, and she offloads half of the stack to me. "Thanks. I know I gave you the rest of the day off, but do you have a minute? I could file these so much faster with another set of hands."

I nod, taking any excuse to stay and look around.

But if Layla is here, I should alert Jace. It's better if she doesn't see his face. I drop the fat pile onto the nearest cabinet and pull out my phone again.

Hang back.

I type out.

"Did you have plans? Don't change them on my account." Layla is watching the phone in my hand.

I tuck it away. "No, it's nothing. This should go quickly between the two of us anyway, right?"

She sets down her own stack and separates them by color. "Yes. Let me explain how this works. The red, yellow, and blue folders are filed by last name. So, find the cabinet that matches the first letter of the last name, and sort it in alphabetical order."

I separate my pile into three different piles: red, yellow, and blue.

"What about the green?" I notice she has a fourth pile.

"These will be filed separately. I'll take care of them." She inches them away from me slightly, pushing them with her long, manicured fingers.

The bolt in the door clicks open, and metal whispers against the thick carpet. Jace. My message either went through too late, or he ignored it. He's got a few files tucked under his arm. Where did those come from? Layla glances at him, and he nods in greeting, then moves across the room and turns his back to us.

Layla turns back to me. "Let's get this sorted." She picks up a few files and walks them to a drawer near me. As she goes through the neatly organized innards, she clears her throat. "This might be nosy, but I don't get much girl talk working here, so I'm dying to ask. Was that a boyfriend you were texting?" She flashes me a hopeful and conspiratorial grin.

My eyes flit to Jace, but I quickly move them back down. My cheeks burn.

"You're totally blushing. It was, wasn't it? Tell me about him." She demands with excitement.

I blow air out my nose. "He's not a boyfriend." I pick up a folder and fiddle with the edges. "Just a guy I met recently. I'm planning on meeting him after this. But it's still early days. I don't know if it's going anywhere or not." Not a lie.

"Okay, fair enough." She continues sorting. "Is he cute?"

The rustling of papers from Jace's direction halts. My whole neck flames. Layla's phone buzzes, and she pulls it out to check the screen. She huffs and straightens. "It's Erebus. He left early, but he's been sending me extra tasks to do all day. I have to run up to his office. I'll be right back, I promise." She shoves her phone in her pocket and stalks out of the room, pulling the door firmly shut behind her.

I consider Layla, her job, and what she must go through working here. How does she stand it? How can she keep watch while other girls are taken into his den? My stomach twists. I know I'm not any better. I'm acutely aware of the monster that he is, and I've never said a word.

Jace appears at my side. "Where do we check first?"

I need to focus. We don't have long. "We're looking for Hamill. It should be in the cabinet marked H." I guide him over to it and pull out the top drawer. We both look at the tabs, gliding over the names as swiftly as possible, pulling forward each folder on the rack with our fingertips.

"So, what were you going to answer?"

"Hmm?"

"Were you going to tell her that I'm cute?" That smile of his hitches up at the corner.

I jab him hard in the ribs with my elbow.

He grunts at the impact then laughs.

"Get a room." Ian grumbles through the earpiece.

That just makes Jace laugh more. The smile drops off his face when he reaches the middle of the drawer. "There's no Hamill here. It would be between these two names, but there's nothing."

He's right. It's missing. Misplaced? Or maybe...

I run to the stack of green files. I start sifting through them but stop when my eyes land on a name I recognize. My name.

I pull the file towards me. Jace is quick to follow and continues looking through the rest of the pile. He notices I've stopped. "Is that it?" he asks hopefully.

"No." I open it. My picture is paper-clipped to several other documents. Grades from school, doctor evaluations, records of employment. The last page holds a picture of a much younger Sariah. Stamped over the top of my head in bold red letters is one word: *SEER*.

"Got it." Jace announces. The name Demelza Hamill winks from the middle of the stack.

The deadbolt clicks, and my heart jumps into my throat. I slam down my folder, sweeping all the green files back into a neat pile. Jace takes a few steps back to distance himself from me. When Layla walks back in, I'm picking up a yellow folder from my own pile.

"Were you leaving? Here you go." Layla holds the door aloft for Jace to exit. He stands there for half a second, considering. I sense he doesn't like the idea of leaving me here alone, but he knows as well as I do dispute will raise suspicion. He nods to Layla again and leaves, turning the corner and disappearing.

"Sorry about that. Let's get this done so you're not late for your date." Layla picks up the green files and carries them to the cabinet just right of the door.

"Did you get it?" Ian's voice crackles to life in my ear.

"No," Jace replies under his breath.

I watch Layla. "So, the green ones go in the cabinet to the right of the door. In the second drawer? Are they done alphabetically too?"

She stops and looks back at me over her shoulder. "Yes. But like I said before, you won't have to worry about the green ones."

My phone vibrates. I take it out to read the message.

How long should I wait before creating a diversion?

"Is that him? I don't want to keep you. Really, you should go have fun. I'll take care of this. Let me walk you out." Without leaving me time to reply, she closes her drawer and opens the door again.

"Um, yeah. Okay." I type out a rushed message to Jace.

> Car now.

A second later, Jace is in my ear again. "Garage clear, Ian?"

"Clear."

I drop the yellow folder back on the pile, sucking in a gasp as the edge slices deep into the pad of my forefinger. I press the paper cut against my thumb to hold back the blood. I make a show of patting my pockets to ensure I have all my belongings, buying another second of time to think. There's no way I can grab the file without her noticing.

"Everything okay?"

"Yes," I say, turning to follow her out. "Coming."

"Which way did you come in?"

"I used the garage." We turn that direction. The sweat from before has turned cold, chilling my skin.

"This is going to sound terrible, but I'm glad you're here, Sariah." Layla's gaze is downcast. "The other girls don't talk to me. They hate me. And I know that might change for you. I'm sure it will. But it's nice to have someone to be friendly with. Not that I'm saying we're friends, I mean—"

"No," I jump in. "I know what you mean. I feel the same way. Copeland's got his claws in all of us. I'm sure you're not immune."

Layla gives me a tight smile.

As we walk, Layla tells me about her pet cat. I focus on the details of how she found it in the alley behind her apartment, and not on the new perspiration forming under my armpits.

She's telling me what a picky eater little Agnes is when we make it to the end of the garage. "Listen to me going on and on. Sorry. I obviously need some other friends. I'll let you go. Which car is yours?"

"That silver station wagon. I bought it used and got a great deal. Figured it would be a sound investment with the new job." Look at the rehearsed lie coming in handy.

"That's great! Well, you'd better go. Have a fun time tonight." She waves and starts to leave, but when she looks over at the station wagon, she stiffens. She grabs my hand and takes a few steps back, pulling me with her.

"What's wrong?" All the hairs on my arms raise.

She turns back to me and whispers, "There's someone in your car."

THIRTY

I can't breathe.

Layla pulls out her phone to call security. Did she see Jace? Or Ian?

"Hello, Franklin, we need a guard in the garage now."

The back door on the other side of the car flies open, making us both jump. Ian sprints past the few other cars, gunning for the garage exit. He hops the low wall in a fluid hurdle, landing on his feet and running out of view. Layla grips my hand so tight it hurts. The other back door pops open, and she screams.

Jace exits the car slowly, raising his hands above his head. He glances at me before looking down, but I can't tell what he's thinking. Ian's breath puffs through the earpiece, heavy from exertion, then it cuts out with a burst of static. The connection is dead.

We've messed up. It's over.

By the time a guard reaches us, I'm shaking all over. The guard slaps a pair of cuffs onto Jace's wrists, shoving him back towards the building. Layla tells the guard what happened, and he calls in backup, assuring us they will find whoever it was that ran away. She leads me inside after Jace and the guard, with an arm around my shoulders.

"I am so sorry, Sariah, I swear, this is highly unusual. We have security measures in place. This should never have happened. We will make sure you get home safely." Layla herds me into an empty office as Jace disappears down the hall. She pulls her phone out again, holding it to her ear. "We'll get to the bottom of this." She says to me.

I wring my shaking hands, trying and failing to regain my composure. At least she'll blame it on the shock for now, assume I'm frightened there were strangers in my car. I clear my throat. "I'd like to use the restroom. I need a minute to collect myself," I whisper to Layla. She nods and mouths, "Of course." I exit into the hallway. The nearest restroom lies at the end of the hall, and I beeline for it. Inside, I duck my head to check under each of the stalls. Empty.

Something shifts in my periphery, and my head snaps to catch the movement. But it's only my reflection.

The woman in the mirror looks frazzled. Her blonde hair sits limp against her shoulders, her complexion has turned sickly, and her gray eyes stretch wide with pink lines creeping across the whites. I approach her and grip the sink. I'm used to seeing the pain etched into the lines at the corners of my eyes, but there's something new there too. A light that wasn't there before. The faintest glimmer of hope. Perhaps that's what is making me hurt so much in this moment. I cast my eyes down. A wad of paper towels clogs half the drain — lifeless, drenched, and forgotten. The hard, cold porcelain provides just enough support to keep me from curling in on myself.

Ian is gone for now, but they could catch him. Jace is in custody. Who knows what they'll be able to get out of him? And there's a high likelihood I'll never get my hands on Demelza's file again. I'll have nothing. I yank the dead earpiece out of my ear and stuff it in my pocket. I knew it was pointless to hope. I'm never going to escape this awful town.

Not only that. I've failed the only people who have ever really needed me.

My heart sinks.

I turn on the tap to splash water on my face. I notice the drop of blood oozing from the paper cut only as it reaches the running water.

THE SILENCE STIFLES ME, weighing down the air. It breaks with a crack as a single spot of flame dances to life, piercing the darkness.

Damp seeps through the knees of my pants.

I rake my fingers over the ground, aching to understand my surroundings. Soft black dirt.

The sky above is ebony and starless.

As my eyes adjust to the flame, a prickle crawls over my brain. There is a presence here.

I let my eyes roam, not daring to speak a word. Beyond the flame, something comes into focus. Steps rising from the soil, leading to a throne. Upon it sits a figure shrouded in a black veil that rests on the top of its head and extends to its feet.

A magnetic sensation pulls at my chest, like an anchor has

lodged into my ribcage and its chain is dragging me towards the figure. It takes everything in me not to move. The pain is searing, my head throbbing from the tension.

I wait silently. My whole body grows heavier the longer I sit, fighting the pull, staring at the dark figure. After a stretch of time, the flame goes out, and I fall.

THE SINK IS OVERFLOWING, spilling onto my shoes. I regain my senses and slam down the tap, reeling away until my back presses against the stall behind me. A buzzing against my leg makes me jolt. I dig for my phone and put it to my ear.

"Hello," I choke past the dryness in my throat.

"Sariah, where are you? I've been calling and calling. You disappeared. I thought you said you needed to use the bathroom! Did the man find you? Are you okay?" Layla's voice climbs octaves on the other end of the line, the last word so shrill I pull my ear away.

"I'm okay. I'm in the bathroom. It took a little longer than I expected to settle myself." One look at my reflection in the mirror makes it clear I am still far from settled.

"A little longer? We've been searching for you for six hours!" A smack echoes as the door to the bathroom flies open and Layla storms in, pocketing her phone with a sigh of relief. She throws her arms around me and sobs. It only takes seconds for her to right herself, wiping away the show of emotion. "Are you okay, really?"

"Yes, I'm okay." I repeat. I can't believe it's been six hours. "I guess I passed out from the stress." I try to conjure up an excuse for my absence, but it falls flat.

"Well, you're here now. I am relieved you are safe." Layla's phone rings again, and she picks up. "Go, Franklin, I'm listening." A long pause ensues while she listens to the head of security. "You are supposed to call me with good news. Get this situation under control. I've got her, and we will be there shortly." She puts the phone away and assesses me.

"What is it?" I tense. Did they catch Ian?

"They are still looking for the individual who ran from your car. The other one is in holding. Do you feel up to coming along? Maybe you'll recognize him, and we can figure out what he was doing." My stomach drops to my feet. Will I be able to lie my way out of this?

"Yes, I'll come." Of course I'll come. I have to learn what they plan to do to him.

She nods and guides me out of the bathroom. My wet feet squelch against the slick floors of the hall, all the way to the security wing. I pick at my finger, noticing the dark soil stuck under my nails.

Why did I ask for Jace's help? I should have done this alone. It's my fault that he is here, that they captured him. He trusted me too much.

A tall, heavyset man waits for us. Layla takes him aside. I can't hear what he says, but when they finish conversing, she leads me to a door and tells me to look through the small window. Sure enough, Jace sits alone at a metal table. He looks exhausted, fatigue

pulling at the lines of his face, his lips turned down in pained con-
centration. Have they had him sitting here shackled to a table for six
hours?

"Do you recognize him?" Layla asks.

I shake my head, eyes still on Jace, studying the way his dark
hair falls over his brow. Seeing him so alone, so helpless, I steel myself.

"Has anyone questioned him yet?" I look back at Layla. I
need to get a grip on this situation.

"He hasn't said a word," she growls. "And thanks to Erebus,
our building doesn't have security cameras. We can't check to see
how he broke into the parking garage." Her nails clack against the
phone in her hand as she grinds her teeth.

"What will happen to him?" I try my best not to seem too
eager. Keep my tone even. I'm surprised she doesn't recognize him
from the records room. But if she's not going to bring it up, neither
am I.

"We'll move him to holding tonight and keep him there
until he talks. Don't you worry, Sariah, we won't let him near you."
Layla grips my forearm for a moment. "Do you need somewhere to
stay? Or will you be safe going home?"

"I'll go home and get some rest," I reply, glancing through
the glass again. I can go to Marshall's. If Ian sticks to the plan, that's
where he should be. We can regroup. I hate to leave Jace alone, but
I have no way to reach him. We'll have to sneak back in later, make
a new plan, set up a watch to see if they move him, or —

"Sure. I'll send one of our guards on your tail so there are
no more problems." Layla brushes past me to speak with Franklin

again.

Her words hit me like a slap to the face.

My whole body goes cold.

I have to go back home.

THIRTY-ONE

BREATHE. COME ON, BREATHE. I peek at the car in the rearview mirror for the hundredth time since leaving the parking garage. My chest feels like it's full of shrapnel, and I can only suck shallow gasps of air between my lips. The lack of sleep and oxygen makes me dizzy, and I grip the steering wheel harder, my knuckles turning white.

Jace is stuck. Ian is on the run all alone. Demelza's file is still in the records room. And now I have to face Audrey. All the muscles in my back clench. She's going to be furious. I've been trying to figure out why she hasn't reported my leaving to Copeland yet. Probably to save face. But once she has me alone, I have no doubt she'll rip into me for running off.

I turn into the driveway, the guard parking on the curb in front of the house. He doesn't get out. I force a strangled breath to fill my lungs.

One breath. In. Out.

No more time to delay. I open the car door and turn to offer him a stiff wave.

He doesn't leave.

I dig my house keys out of my purse and walk around to the garage side door. Guess I won't be making a run for it.

Audrey's car is in the garage. She's home. I enter the house slowly, fighting the fear that seizes my heart.

It takes only ten steps to make it to the kitchen. It's not the first time I've counted, but the route feels foreign now, like I don't belong here anymore. Although if I'm honest, I never truly felt I belonged here.

Now I understand why. I've lived my life in a stranger's house, playing pretend. I was the perfect doll, doing as I was told.

Don't talk back, Sariah.

Smile, Sariah, you need to make a good impression.

Lighten up, Sariah. Don't be so sensitive.

Every correction, every dig, followed up with a vie for connection.

I say it because I care about you.

I worry about you.

I see how special you are.

"Look who decided to come home." Audrey stands near the stove, mug in hand, blowing at the steam rising from her drink. She takes in my disheveled appearance, lips pursed, eyes tight. She sets the mug down and draws a slow breath, her face melting into a sad smile. Her arms open wide as she strolls over to wrap me in a hug, and squeezes my rigid form. "I have been so worried about you. You have not answered your phone in days. Where have you been?" Her hands come to my shoulders, and she pushes away to hold me at arm's length, searching my face, calculating something.

What am I even supposed to say?

"I've been busy. The new job is... demanding." Now it's my

turn to watch. Once again, I'm on a board, surveying the squares. Her move.

"Yes, Erebus told me you were coming in. You put me in a difficult position, Sariah. I had to lie for you. I trusted that if you were in trouble, you would come to me. You know I am always here for you, dear." Her earlier question still hangs in the air between us, dripping with guilt-infused honey. Do I take the bait? What alternative do I have?

"You didn't need to do that. The new job pays well. I went ahead and put a payment down on that apartment. The one I was looking at before. I bought myself a car too. It's parked in the drive-way." I bluff, nodding my head in that direction.

As I suspected, she bristles. Her eyebrows draw together for just a fraction of a second before the calm façade returns. "How generous of Erebus. I told you taking that job was in your best interest, didn't I? Although, I'm guessing you did not tell him about your new living arrangements. He's reiterated how important it is for you to be home, where I can be here to help you. You know how you have your episodes. I understand this must feel exciting, but we need to talk this through." She takes a seat on one of the barstools at the counter and pats her hand on the one beside her.

Heat rises inside me.

Now that I've discovered the reality of our situation, I have questions of my own.

I sit facing the counter, watching my fingers pick at my nail beds so I don't have to look her in the eye while I talk. "He was okay with it, actually. Had his assistant help me set it up. They seem close.

She's taken me under her wing."

"His assistant? You mean Layla?" Her tone is sharp.

"You know her?"

"Yes." She drums her fingertips on the countertop. I glance over and watch her process this development.

"How long have you worked for the commissioner, Mom?" I force out the last word.

The question catches her off guard. "About thirty years, I suppose. And call him Erebus, dear, he's a friend, not just an employer."

"So, you've known everyone in his office then, I bet. Do you remember a Demelza Hamill?" I press.

Her eyes snap to mine. "Where did you hear that name?"

I've struck a nerve. She knows something. If I can't get to the file, a firsthand account may get me sufficient answers.

"I overheard Erebus talking about her to Layla. He seemed really concerned about her. I only caught a snippet, but it sounded like she used to work in the office too?" I count on her urge to gossip to take over.

Audrey huffs. "Yes, that tramp used to work for him. We were on a team together before she abandoned our project. Took half the research with her when she did."

"She was a doctor?" Now that the gates are open, I must keep her talking.

"Ha! No. Demelza's people skills were lacking, to put it mildly. Not someone you'd want to work with patients. She was a researcher in the lab. It's hardly important, but one day she and

Erebus got into a big fight, and the next thing we knew she was gone. It took us months to get back on track. No regard for the rest of us. I, for one, am glad she left." Audrey pats down an invisible hair, smoothing it into her perfect bun.

"Gone, huh? And no one knows where she went?"

"No." She looks me up and down, squinting. "Anyway, back to the matter at hand. What have you been doing at your new apartment without any of your things? Is that why you came back here? To pack?" Again, she conjures up that sad face, like I have betrayed her, and she wants me to see how much it pains her.

"No actually. I was stalked at work today. A man followed me into the garage, so a guard escorted me here. It was probably nothing, but you know how careful the commissioner — Erebus — likes to be. Insisted I be accompanied home. The whole situation upset him. He asked me if you were free. I think he wanted to see you." I dangle the carrot.

She sits up straighter. "If Erebus wants to see me, he knows how to call me. What do you mean you were stalked?" Gates closed. She's shifted focus.

"It was nothing." I evade. "Since you brought it up, I think I will go start packing." I stand and start to walk out of the kitchen. When I reach the hall, she laughs. A mirthless sound, low in her throat.

"Sariah." She waits for me to turn around. "You really think you can lie to me?" Any ounce of sadness has vanished, her expression that of a cat ready to pounce. My whole body goes tight, bracing for the onslaught. "I raised you. No one else knows you like I do. You saw Demelza, didn't you? You know something and you are trying to keep it a secret."

I could deny it, stick to my story. But the anger bubbling up in my gut boils into hot, blinding rage. The words come out barely louder than a whisper. "You want to talk about secrets? How about the one where you pretended I was your daughter, but really, I'm just some twisted experiment?" Tears rim my eyes, blurring my vision.

I tried to ignore it when Jace and Ian first broke the news, but her betrayal runs deeper than I want to admit. Like a whole piece of me is torn away. The woman who bandaged my scrapes and iced my bruises. The one who held me when I cried. The one who brought home my favorite donuts just because she knew I liked them. Yes, it's all mingled in with the endless psychiatric evaluations, the pointed judgments and comments, and allowing Copeland to use me at his whim, but it's the only love I've known, and seeing the cold emptiness in her eyes now, it's clear that none of it was real.

"Look who smartened up. Little Sariah, all grown, thinks she knows everything." Audrey's lips curl into an icy smile, spitting the words like venom.

My hands are shaking now. Slowly, I inch towards the stove, putting the kitchen island between us. I won't hold back anymore. I strike where I know it will hurt. "Copeland has never cared about you. He will never love you. He will never be with you. He will never choose you. Using me will never get you what you want, so why don't we just drop the charade?"

Her pupils darken with fury. In a fraction of a second, the air shifts with her seething. The game has changed, and I no longer know what to expect from my opponent. I'm ready for her words, for her to raise her voice, for her tears to fall like a raging storm of vitriol.

What I don't expect is her charging over the countertop with a feral scream. She lunges at me with speed I never would have believed her to be capable of.

Before I can process what is happening, her hands have clawed into my shirt, pulling my face close to hers, her breath hot on my face. There are no words, only frenzied wails. She's shaking me back and forth, forcing me against the counter. My head hits the cabinet behind me, the sharp pain sending holes across my vision.

My hands fly out in an effort to steady myself. I hit something that screeches against the stovetop. Instinctively, I pat around to locate the object, eyes glued to the horror show that has taken over. My fingers close around a solid metal handle.

I don't think.

I just swing as hard as I can.

THIRTY-TWO

THE SICKENING THUMP TURNS my stomach, bringing me back to my senses.

Audrey crumples to the ground at my feet, my fist tight around the pan's handle. Chest heaving, the air through my nostrils is suddenly the loudest sound in this eerily quiet space.

What have I done?

I'm scared to touch her. Scared to move at all.

A full minute passes before I crouch down, so slowly. I carefully reach out two shaking fingers to feel for the pulse in her neck. I think I feel something, but I could be doing it wrong, and my own heart is hammering so hard I may just be feeling my own blood shooting through my fingertips. I draw them back and watch her torso instead. There's a slight rise and fall.

Once.

Twice.

She's breathing.

She's alive.

My shoulders fall just an inch.

What if she wakes up? After what I just witnessed, I believe she could kill me. I should leave now. If I sneak out the back, I can scale the wall. It will take ages to get to Marshall's on foot, but the guard won't see me. Assuming that's truly the only guard sent to keep an eye on me. Unfortunately, I can't be sure. Copeland may not allow cameras, but he's got eyes everywhere, and I'm still a mess from everything that has transpired over the last seven hours. I stand and my eyes flit to the glowing numbers on the stove. 2:00 am.

A glimmer of an idea passes through my mind.

A risky, irrational idea.

I bound over Audrey's limp body and rush for her closet. The dark and the cold are in my favor. Selecting pants, a shirt, a jacket, and shoes—all black—I strip as fast as I can and change. I dig around for the thickest scarf she owns, wrapping it around my neck repeatedly to hide the lower half of my face. Audrey never wears hats.

Moving to her vanity, I rake her brush over my hair, pulling it back into a severe bun, securing it with an elastic and pins as fast as I can manage. It's not perfect, but it will have to suffice. As an added measure, I pull her brown trench coat off its hanger and throw it on as I exit the room, pulling up on the collar to shield my face even more.

She may not be my biological mother, but Copeland certainly found a fake who looked similar enough to me to avoid my suspicion. Catching sight of myself in the mirror, my heart skips a beat. If I don't look into my eyes, I could be her. This could work, but I have to move fast.

I only need a few minutes head start to lose him.

One breath. In. Out.

Her purse hangs on its hook by the garage. I trust that the

keys will be inside. Everything in its place, as always. My own purse still rests discarded on the floor here, and I move to tuck it under the long coat when a buzzing sound erupts from Audrey's bag. I crouch low, hiding even though no one can see me here.

I gingerly unzip the bag and slide Audrey's phone from a slim pocket. The screen glows, a name in white letters splayed under the glass: *Layla Bramwell*. The buzzing ends and the screen goes black.

Layla was checking up on me, and Audrey just missed her call. Will she send the guard in to check on us now? My chest constricts at the thought. I jump when the text message comes in.

> Checking in. Is Sariah still with you?

Maybe I can still salvage this. Piecing together my next moves in my head, I type.

> Yes. She is shaken. I'm leaving to the 24-hour store to get her something to calm down. Keep the guard posted outside. I won't be long.

It's a gamble, but I don't give myself a chance to second-guess it. I tuck Audrey's bag and my own under my arm and wait one beat before opening the door into the garage.

Then my stomach drops.

I parked the station wagon in the driveway. Audrey's car is blocked in. The guard will be suspicious of her taking my car, won't he? Even if Layla just instructed him to remain by the house, will he call it in? Or worse, will he go into the house to check on me?

Maybe it all depends on how much Layla trusts Audrey. Obviously, the only way to leave is to drive the station wagon. It's a valid excuse for her to borrow it. Audrey clearly does not like the commissioner's assistant, but that doesn't mean she hasn't charmed her like she does everyone else.

I stop debating with myself and move.

I hit the switch to open the garage door, and it lurches with a deep groan.

Confidence, walk with confidence. I am Audrey Invidia, and I have a patient to tend to. Nothing will get in my way.

One foot in front of the other, I draw the car keys from my bag. My eyes flick to the guard against my will, searching behind the windshield. Too dark to see. I ignore the tired ache of my body, the dull cramping in my abdomen, as I drag the car door open and climb into the driver's seat. I slam the door locked as soon as I'm inside. My fingers tremble as I dig around to find the remote in Audrey's purse, but I manage to locate it and press the button. Then, I turn the key in the ignition and slowly reverse onto the street as the garage door meets the ground.

The guard's car lies dormant. No headlights, no rumbling engine. I drive away as controlled as I can manage, pressing harder on the gas pedal once I round the corner. If he does follow me, there's not much I can do about it, so I switch my focus.

The goal now is to find Ian. Please, please be at Marshall's.

This time of night is unsettling, morphing every tree and lamppost into predators. My eyelids weigh a ton but are glued open. I've been lucky so far, managing escape, but I know how odds work.

I won't get a chance like this again.

Shadows fill the windows of the store. It will stay quiet for another hour or two. Where would Ian go? I swing the car into the back parking lot and shut it off. Without the hum of the engine, I feel terribly exposed.

Both my and Audrey's bags lie splayed on the passenger seat. I haven't noticed anyone on my tail, but now I wonder if I should keep her phone with me or try to get rid of it. Mine was bugged and tracked. Hers must be as well, right? So many questions. Always another puzzle, always another frustrating piece of the game to unravel.

Now that I'm alone, a hollow ache takes over my insides. What would it be like to live without fear? Without a threat lurking at every corner? Without constantly looking over my shoulder? The notion is beyond my imagination.

Stupid hot tears have filled my eyes again, and I lower the visor mirror to clean my face. A photograph greets me instead. Inside the weathered edges, five people smile at me. Two adults I've never seen. A baby that must be Vanessa. A younger Ian. And Jace. Younger too, but his blue eyes are unmistakable. I lean in for a better look. The blue eyes are his, but they are also different. Void of so much pain and gravity.

I'm not the only one the commissioner has hurt. Not the only future he stole.

A tap on the window sends my head flying back, whacking against the headrest. It takes my eyes a moment to adjust, but when I recognize Ian's face under his hood, I exhale in relief.

I unlock the doors and motion for him to go around.

"You're here." I declare when he pulls the passenger door shut behind him.

"So are you." His voice shakes.

"How long have you been waiting? I'm sorry it took me so long."

He swallows. "Once I got out of the building, I ran through town. I stopped to hide along the way to check if anyone was following me. I got to the store about five hours ago. There are some bushes there." He points to a small patch of shrubbery against the wall outside. "It was dark enough that I was able to sit behind it without anyone noticing."

Five hours alone in the dark, crouching behind a bush. I nearly start crying again. Instead, I open the middle console, looking for something, anything, and find a stray granola bar. I offer it to him, but he shakes his head.

"Where is Jace?" Ian pales, noticing that his brother isn't with us. "What happened?"

My mouth opens, but the words die on my tongue. Ian shouldn't be here. He shouldn't have to put himself at risk. If the commissioner caught an inkling that Ian has dreams too, there would be nothing to stop him from using Ian as an experiment. He's still just a kid. I can't let that happen. "I'm taking you home." I finally say. I reach to turn the keys again, but Ian is faster, yanking them out of the ignition.

"What happened?" He yells this time, the keys clinking together in his hand.

I grip the wheel, my knuckles turning white. "They have Jace. He didn't make it out. They sent a guard with me, but I was able to get away. I think." I glance at each of the mirrors to check behind us. "I promise I came as soon as I could. But I shouldn't have asked you to help. Now Jace is stuck, and we didn't even get the file. It was a reckless idea. You should go—"

Ian reaches under his hoodie and slides out a green folder.

My whole body freezes. "What is that?" I whisper.

"It's Demelza's file. I looked at it, and it must be her. The picture is just how you described her, the red hair and everything. She was a scientist. It says she worked with Copeland until about fifteen years ago."

Dumbstruck, I stare at the green folder. "How?"

"Jace." Ian shrugs. "As soon as he left, he texted me about where it was. We thought I could take a turn. He handed me the key card when he got back to the car. But you followed him out so quickly there wasn't time to try. I've been studying the schematics of the building for ages, so when I ran, I went straight to a maintenance entrance and used the cloned card to get in. No one was around the records room, probably because all the security was in the garage at that point, so I swiped it and got out as fast as I could." He finishes his story with a shrug, like what he did was no big deal, but there is also an underlying sense of pride in his words.

I muster a smile. "You did good, Ian. That is incredible." We have the file. We have our intel.

But we don't have Jace.

"So, what now?" Ian asks.

My phone rings in my purse, making me jump. I scoop it out of my bag. Layla's number appears, so I answer. "Layla? Is everything okay?"

They found Audrey. They know what I did. They've tracked her phone here, and they're going to find me and arrest me, and I just dragged Ian into all of this as an accomplice.

"Yes, everything is okay. I have good news and bad news. Unfortunately, the man we took into custody still won't talk. But we are transferring him into custody with the official guard. They will move him in an hour. You won't have to worry about him anymore." There is an expectant silence.

I try to match her upbeat tone. "Oh. Good. Where are they moving him?"

"To the disciplinary facility across town. But he is already in a squad car waiting to leave. We will finish the paperwork, then he'll be out of your hair."

My fingers are ice around the curved edges of the phone. "Okay, thank you, Layla." I end the call and look at Ian. "Jace needs us. They're moving him to the prison. If we leave now, we might be able to reach him before they leave the office." What I'm saying is crazy. I have no idea how we can get him away from the police at this point, but I'll hate myself if I don't try.

Ian doesn't question me further. He extends his hand and offers me the keys.

THIRTY-THREE

THE COLD SILENCE WHEN I kill the engine sends bile into my throat. I glance at Ian and see his eyes are wide, jaw clenched. We're a few blocks away from the parking garage. The walk shouldn't take long, but I don't trust these streets. If I thought we could get away with it, I'd pull into the parking garage. But Layla knows the station wagon now. We'll go on foot.

I clear the knot in my throat with a cough, and nod at Ian. We both open our doors, which creak on their old hinges. I shut mine as gently as possible, but Ian throws his closed, taking long strides towards the office building. I'm forced to jog to catch up with him.

"Ian, wait! We should scope things out before we barge in." I whisper at him. There's no way he can't hear me, but he doesn't acknowledge me, just keeps his gaze ahead. I've seen that look before, only the last time it was on his brother, when Jace was surrounded by a whole pack of guys hoping to beat him senseless.

But we're not facing a group of drunk losers. These guards and officers are armed. Trained. With the means to lock us away for good or execute us on command.

I grab his arm and drag him into the shadows, forcing him to look at my face. "Ian, I know you're scared, but we have to think this through. I want to save him too, but if we play this wrong, we could all end up dead." He doesn't deny being scared, though he ducks his head.

He heaves a breath. "I told you before, this was never your fight. You can walk away. I'll take care of my family." With hands shoved deep into his pockets, he rolls his shoulders back, standing tall.

My head shakes. "Copeland has held my life in his palm from day one. There is nowhere for me to go." Nowhere in this town at least. "We're doing this together."

He looks down at me and nods once.

"Stay close to the walls. Don't let anyone see you." We continue our walk, my head on constant swivel.

Every window is dark. Only half of the street lamps emit their yellow glow, casting puddles of light randomly over the sidewalk. Something is not right. I've gone home at this hour before, and there are usually a handful of stragglers walking around. The late bus should still be rolling through town. But I don't see a single person, not a single moving vehicle.

Maybe I'm just being jumpy. I should be grateful the guard from my house hasn't found me yet. And that Layla isn't calling me, demanding to know where I am and how Audrey ended up knocked out on the kitchen floor.

If we can get to Jace, I can take us somewhere else, somewhere Copeland can't follow us. I could transport us to Sophia's cabin again. She can help us make a plan or at least give us somewhere safe to stay while we figure out how to get to Vanessa.

When we turn the final corner, artificial white light oozes from the parking garage, a blinding contrast to the looming exterior of the building against the black sky.

One breath. In. Out.

At least there aren't cameras to dodge. We sprint across the street, my heart screaming at me for exposing my body to empty space, nothing to hide behind. It calms to a quick thud as we crawl into the shrubbery lining the building, pounding deep in my ears.

Ian and I both take a moment to lean against the cement half-wall wrapped around the garage and catch our breath.

He nudges me and raises three fingers. He mouths the words as he drops each of them back to his palm. Three, two, one.

We rise just enough to see above the barrier. There aren't many vehicles scattered throughout the space. But a whole line of police cars fills the spots closest to the building. Jace must be in one of them. The question is, will he be alone?

Walking straight across the garage would be suicidal. How else can we get a closer vantage point?

Ian is already on his hands and knees, crawling over the dirt to round the corner. From the wall next to the cars, we should be able to see in the side windows. I get down and follow behind him, shielding my eyes from the dust he's kicking up.

When we get close, I peek over the wall again. Jace's head is visible in the backseat of the car closest to our wall. No one occupies the front seat, and the driver's side window is rolled down. Why would they leave it rolled down? It's freezing out here. Are they forgetful or trying to be cruel? I crane my neck, trying to tell if anyone occupies the other cars.

The movement must catch Jace's eye because he turns to look at me. Tape covers his mouth, but his eyes grow wide. He starts shaking his head hard and fast. What is that supposed to mean?

"Do you see anyone else?" I whisper to Ian.

"No. They all look empty. We should go now before they come out here." He doesn't wait for me to answer, just stands, and hops over the low wall so he can rush to the car.

Too late to turn back now.

I swing a leg over the wall, less efficiently than he did, but after a moment I clear the barrier and join him. Jace still shakes his head at us through the window.

"What are you doing?" I hiss at Ian. He has snaked his hand inside the driver's door.

"I'm unlocking the car." The click is soft but sends a jolt through me. I pull Jace's door open and move to kneel beside him.

His hands are in front of him, zip-tied together with thick black plastic. But his feet are free. He mumbles something, words smothered behind the tape. I reach up to rip it off, wincing along with him.

"Run." Jace croaks.

Ian is up in an instant. He grabs each of us by the arm and yanks us clear of the car. He hops the wall again with ease, turning to grab Jace's bound hands. Jace takes the help, half muscling over, half letting Ian drag him. I scramble to follow them as they find their feet and break into a sprint.

I stumble out of the bushes, the long trench coat catching in the branches. With a hard yank, I free it and run. The brothers are taller and stronger, already eating up so much ground, but I try to keep up.

Until my vision goes black.

THIRTY-FOUR

THE BACK OF MY head throbs. I peel my cheek away from a wooden table, squinting under the fluorescent lights overhead. The square room is bare and gray. It contains only the table at the center, the chair I occupy, and another chair across from me. One metal door is closed on my right. Its small window reveals the white walls of the hall. This must be a holding room. Like the one they had Jace in.

My stomach drops. I didn't make it. They caught me.

Did Jace and Ian get away?

The door opens, and heels click against the tile floor. "Good, you're awake." Layla comes to sit across from me, setting a tall black leather bag down on the table. She fixes me with a guarded stare. "What would you like to explain first?"

They found Audrey. They know I ran away, that I helped the man they had in custody. I have zero possibility of talking my way around things now. But this is Layla. She was the one who told me to run when I had a chance. Will she help me?

"I'm so sorry about Audrey. I didn't mean to hurt her. She attacked me. I hit her before I even realized it was happening." I lean back in my chair and process that cold shackles bind my hands to the table.

"What's this for?" I look to Layla. They can lock the door, so why restrain me?

"Oh, that. Well, we can't have you disappearing again. Not now that we know you can. And as for Doctor Invidia, you did me a favor. Incessant woman. Constantly going on about how we're handling you wrong. She's too caught up in herself to see things our way."

We. Our.

What is she saying?

"You and Copeland, you mean?" My gut twists with the realization. Even if I didn't trust her, the betrayal still hurts.

She just laughs and reaches into the bag. Her long fingernails emerge clutching a green folder. She tosses it onto the table in front of me.

The letters of my name line the tab.

"I'll ask you again, what would you like to explain first? What you were doing with the Boones? Or where your other friends have disappeared to?"

I stare at her, dumbstruck. "What's going on?"

"Oh please, Sariah. You can stop playing games."

I look at her here under these awful lights. She's different than before. Not the overworked, reluctant assistant. Not the conspiratorial friend. This is a woman who knows exactly what she wants and knows she can get it.

"I don't know what you're talking about."

She flips open the file, pointing to the word scrawled across the top of the first page. I read it again: *SEER*.

"Do you deny it?" She asks, raising an eyebrow.

"I don't even know what that means."

"Don't play stupid, Sariah. We're friends, right? Tell me what's been going on. I can help you." She leans back in her chair.

"Friends don't knock their friends out cold," I retort, the back of my head still throbbing.

Layla points again to the file. "You read it, I assume, as well as the others. Where are they?"

Others? The green folders. They must all be for seers. Other people with my ability. That's why Demelza's file was green.

"I didn't read any other files, and I don't know what you're talking about."

She runs a finger over the smooth tabletop, chewing on her next words. "You're the most promising case we've had in decades. We gave the Boones some leash to try things out their own way, but their efforts proved useless. Other subjects have been disappearing, one by one. And then you asked about Demelza Hamill. You know something, Sariah, and you will tell me everything."

Anger festers inside me. Subjects. She views us as a science experiment. But that's insane. She's stuck here too.

"Layla," I choke. "You don't have to be his puppet. You don't have to do what the commissioner tells you anymore. Come with me and we'll leave this place."

She laughs again.

"You think I have time to run around with you and the boys you've collected? That's not how this arrangement works. You report to me, just like Copeland. If you have information, you give it to me. If you don't want to talk, we have other ways of making you cooperate."

My entire world tilts, my brain off-kilter.

"What do you mean, Copeland reports to you? Who do you work for?"

Layla tilts her head to the side, scanning me like she's trying to detect deception. "Let's just say there are higher powers beyond New Harper. And they are extremely interested in what you have to share."

The disgust in my stomach grows as I piece together what she's telling me. "So, what? You offer up girls to Copeland to keep him busy? He's just a flashy shield for you to operate behind?"

Why let him use me if all she wants is information? Tears prick my eyes.

"I allow him to remain a slave to his own desires. It makes him easy to control. You should be happy. Now that we can give up the charade we've been playing, you won't have to deal with him anymore. Let's set the terms so you can understand, shall we?" She shifts in her chair to lean closer. "You can go. Run off with your boys and do whatever it is you've been doing. But when you find answers, you bring them to me. I require the location of the other subjects. Do you understand?"

This doesn't make any sense. "You've read my file. I have vivid dreams. Is that a crime? And as for these others you keep mentioning, I have no idea who you're talking about."

"We both know it's more than dreaming, Sariah. And let's not pretend you're unaware of the Boone children's abilities."

She scrunches her brow in mock concern. "We haven't seen Vanessa in almost a week. We'll keep it simple. You find her, and you lead us to the rest. Can you handle that?"

I consider her words. She'll let me leave. But she already knows more than I do. So why does she need my help?

"Don't worry about the details, Sariah." Can she read my mind? "This is the best offer you'll get."

"Why should I come back? If you let me leave right now, I could stay gone. What makes you assume that I'll work with you?"

"You, Sariah, present an intriguing opportunity. Do not get that confused. You are not essential. If you want a new life, you will follow orders. If you refuse, I will make other arrangements." Her eyes are cold, her words crisp. Layla stands. She leaves my file but slides her bag over one arm. From her blazer pocket, she pulls out a small metal key and tosses it on top of the papers, then heads for the exit. "I'll leave it up to you." She walks out, and the door whispers shut behind her.

THIRTY-FIVE

MY EYES BORE INTO the tiny key, my mind still reeling. Tears fall silently, numbly, down my cheeks. I've been handed everything I ever wanted. A chance to escape this place, to escape Copeland and his control, to go somewhere beyond his reach. And all I want is to puke.

Will I never be free?

That horrible key glints at me, mocking me. I squeeze it between my fingers and unlock the handcuffs, throwing it against the far wall the second they release my wrists. I push back from the table, sending the chair skittering across the floor. My hands rake through my hair, pulling loose the bun. I'm still stuck inside Audrey's suffocating clothes. I unravel the scarf, discarding it on the floor, and brace my hands on the table as I force air into my lungs.

Why is everything a lie? Every single piece of my life.

I should call Layla's bluff. Refuse to cooperate and force her to either lock me up or have me executed.

But I think of Jace. Of all that he's been through. Layla will go after them too, especially if I don't agree to her terms. The difference is they can't get to Vanessa without me. If I don't help them, they'll be stuck here.

They'll be defenseless and clueless about what is really happening.

I can hardly believe Layla knows about them, that the secret family in the woods wasn't so secret after all. Were his parents still working for Copeland's office before they disappeared, despite what Jace said? Did he know?

The thought of him also lying to me sends me flying to the corner of the room to release my measly stomach contents onto the floor in a wet mess. When it's all out, I wipe my mouth across Audrey's sleeve, stumbling back.

What do I do now?

One breath. In. Out.

I can shut myself off. I can shut out every feeling and visualize the puzzle in front of me, study the game board. One move at a time, one piece after the other, I will find a way through this. This is exactly what my life prepared me for.

Carefully, I untangle my hair and smooth it back into a ponytail. I straighten my clothes and turn to walk into the hall. The green file calls for my attention.

I lived my life. Do I need a bunch of papers to verify what I know?

Then again, it appears I don't know anything after all. I scoop up the pages, arrange them neatly, and slide the folder under my arm.

When I open the door, a guard stands waiting.

"Boss said to give you this." He holds a small black box.

I stiffen. "What is it?"

"My orders are to deliver it to you."

Play the game, Sariah. Moves and countermoves. Do whatever it takes to flee this building.

He extends the box to me, and I take it.

"She said to tell you not to lose it." His message delivered, he steps back against the wall and clasps his hands behind his back, moving his eyes away from me.

I don't want to open it, not here, so I slip the box into the trench coat's pocket and stalk away to locate the exit.

Though I try to hide it, I'm still frazzled, and this labyrinth of halls has me walking in circles. When I finally find an exit, the early morning sun greets me with angry power, overwhelmingly bright, and so completely wrong. How can the sun shine on a place like this?

Again, I'm forced to stop and consider my options. Citizens have filled the streets, milling about, heading to work, making last night seem like some awful nightmare.

But where are Jace and Ian? If Layla let me leave, told me to help them, that must mean she let them run. That she meant for me to find them and complete the task of finding Vanessa. Of finding Demelza.

Would they go back to Marshall's? We didn't make backup plans this time.

I walk back towards where I parked the station wagon, not sure where else to go. Dread consumes me when I turn a corner and see that it's still there, empty. I pick up my feet, moving faster. I don't want to attract attention, but I need a closer look. I reach the car and push my face against the window to see inside. No one.

A scraping sound escapes the alley behind me, and I turn on my heel.

"Sariah," Jace whispers. His head peeks out from behind a dumpster, and my shoulders sag in relief. He strides over to me, Ian right behind him. "Are you okay? When we turned around, you were gone. I wasn't sure if you'd vanished again, or if someone had taken you. I didn't know what to do." Jace looks me over, his voice wavering. Red tendrils line the whites of his eyes, setting off the blue. The dark half-moons underneath are a dark and painful-looking purple. He could collapse from exhaustion any second. "We waited. I hoped you'd come back. I'm so glad you came back."

The emotion is too much for me. I shift my gaze to Ian, but that only makes it worse. His eyes are puffy and bright, and his nose is red. He's been crying.

"I'm okay," I lie. "Let's go get Vanessa."

Ian straightens at my words. "Yes." He nods eagerly at my invitation.

Jace steps between us, getting closer to me. "Right now? Are you sure you don't need to recover? We can regroup at the cabin. We still need to see what Demelza's file says, figure out a solid plan." He drops his voice to a whisper. "I thought I lost you."

I allow myself to look at him, to really look. Is he playing games with me? Is this all another lie? Would I even be able to tell?

I want to trust him. But Layla has burdened me with a secret, and until I know for sure that he won't stab me in the back like everyone else, I can't share it with him.

"We don't have time to waste." I say.

Truly, I can't spend one more awful second in New Harper. I start pacing down the alley, worrying my lip between my teeth. They draw blood, and I take action.

"Do either of you have water?" I ask.

Jace hesitates. "Are you sure you're okay?"

"I may never be okay, but I know we have to do this."

He straightens and turns to open the back door. From under the seat, he pulls out a jar of water. They must have stashed containers of the clean water from their stream.

"Both of you take my hands," I instruct. "Jace, you'll give me a sip of that. We're going to get your sister. Whatever you do, don't let go." My body is on the verge of combusting. I want to scream, I want to cry, I want to lie down on the ground and never get up. Instead, I hold out my hands, the coppery taste coating my tongue.

Ian is the first to grab hold, as ready as I am. Jace hesitates again, searching my eyes. He seems to arrive at some conclusion. He twists the lid off the jar and tucks it in a pocket, then takes my other hand.

One breath. In. Out.

My mind fills with the green trees, the girlish laughter, the white dresses, and red hair. I look to Jace, and he lifts the water for me. My lips part to let it mingle with the blood.

THIRTY-SIX

THE HEAT BEATS DOWN on my skin. Have I somehow made a grave mistake? I open my eyes to an expanse of cracked desert sand. A white sun hangs over us like a scythe, promising to end us if we stay here too long. I do know this place. Demelza showed me only briefly, but there is no mistaking it.

My hands still grip my companions. I check that Jace and Ian are intact. Both seem dazed, but neither looks injured. I scan the horizon, trying to find the curtain of light that will lead us to Vanessa. That brilliant, otherworldly veil. Something glints in the distance. I spin a full circle to confirm that light is the only anomaly in this wasteland.

"That way," I direct the brothers. I release their hands and start the trek. They are both quick to follow, and while I can feel their questions buzzing in the air, they don't speak them aloud. The heat has us pulling off our jackets while we walk, sweat pooling over our skin. "Almost there," I promise, the wall of light coming closer into view.

About twenty minutes later, when we've almost reached it, Jace grabs my shoulder.

"Sariah, what's our plan here? We want to help, but you've

got to let us in your head. We don't know what we're walking into."

One breath. In. Out.

"Okay. You remember at Sophia's cabin I was able to lead you in? I believe the same is possible with Hazelgrove. Provided you want to, you should be able to enter with me. Then we'll find your sister, and you can convince her to come with us. I will lead us back out, and we'll go home." My plan relies entirely on conjecture, and I know it.

There is no telling how this passage differs from Sophia's cabin. I expect Demelza will find us as easily as she found me last time. Hopefully, no one else will notice us. If the men stay hidden in the treeline, perhaps one of the other girls will help me locate Vanessa. No one seemed especially hostile. Well, aside from when Demelza clawed my arm.

A pit forms in my cramping stomach. This was a bad idea.

Another in a long succession.

The longer we stand under the harsh sun, the more the ache of exhaustion grows in my bones. I shove it from my mind. It's my responsibility to get us out of here, no matter how tired I may be.

"Let's do it," Ian says. "You lead the way." His hair is plastered to his forehead, wet with sweat, cheeks red. Even after all the setbacks we've faced in the last twenty-four hours, he's ready to trust me with his life. I don't deserve it. I worry I'll disappoint him again.

I look to Jace. His lips are dry and starting to crack. "I'll always follow you." He says.

The words make me feel worse. He trusts a version of me that doesn't exist. At least not yet. That is, if I choose to believe everything he's told me is true.

I center myself between them again, and we link hands.

It only takes a second to step through to Hazelgrove, but it feels like an eternity as I squeeze their fingers. I remember Demelza saying no man could pass the veil, but I refuse to be stopped. A guttural cry escapes me as I pull us into the cool embrace of the forest.

Once in the trees, I fall to my knees, gasping. I can hear them both on the ground behind me. We made it. I did it.

I turn to them, victory surging through me, but something is wrong. Both writhe on the forest floor, suddenly pale, their breaths rushing in ragged spurts.

"What's wrong?" I rush to their sides, looking between the two.

"It hurts," Jace forces the words through clenched teeth. "Everything hurts." He pushes against the ground, but collapses. "I can't move."

Ian doesn't speak. His eyes scrunch tightly closed, tears escaping at the corners.

"Go. Find her." Jace chokes out.

I watch helplessly for a second more, but he's right. Their relief requires leaving. But we can't leave without Vanessa. Not when we've risked so much already.

Forcing myself to move, I leave them at the veil and lurch into the trees. My feet itch to run, to get this over with quickly. But every copse of trees looks identical, and I can't gain my bearings. I trudge forward, dragging my coat behind me, straining my ears for any hint of the women who live here.

After an eternity, a gap appears in the trees. I race for it, tumbling onto a dirt path. It's the corridor of homes. The handmade buildings greet me on either side of the walkway. Every window is dark, and the settlement is quiet. Memories of last night threaten me, pressing down on my chest, but I stay focused.

I walk past the last house, and a sound finally finds me. It's faint, but I recognize it. The chanting.

From here I can remember the route, following the path that runs along the river. As I near the voices, I break off into the trees for cover. The circle of girls in the meadow has grown. More people have joined. How has Demelza recruited more women in a matter of days?

I push the question aside when I see her. Long dark hair rests against the white nightgown, paces in front of where I stand. Vanessa's back is to me.

I take my gaze off her to search for Demelza. It takes only a moment to locate her red curls. She's meandering around a fire lit in the center of the meadow, her eyes on the flames. This is my shot. I discard my coat on the ground to free up my hands. When Demelza is looking the other way, I step past the tree line, raising my arms, treading as lightly as I can manage. I wrap a hand over Vanessa's mouth and an arm around her waist, pulling hard to yank her into the cover of the trees. She struggles against my grip, but I'm larger than her, and I refuse to let go. I knock her feet out from under her so I can drag her. She claws at my arms, at the hand over her mouth, her cries of protest just muffled enough under the sound of the chanting. I carry her as far away from the group as I can before my arms give out, barely earning the cover of the greenery, then force her to the ground, still covering her mouth so she can't scream.

I listen to hear if anyone followed us. The other women and girls continue to chant. When I'm satisfied we're alone, I turn my face to her. She looks up at me and goes rigid. She waits, now still. Slowly, I pull my hand away from her mouth.

"You look just like the drawings." She whispers.

"Vanessa," I pant, winded from the exertion, "you need to come with me."

"Where?" Her small frame trembles.

"Your brothers. They're here. They want you to come home."

She shakes her head. "That's impossible. They can't be here."

"They're here. But they're in pain. We have to go now."

Her mouth opens, but any argument dies on her lips, and she pushes herself up to follow me. I retrieve the coat, and we move swiftly. I must trust that she'll come along to see her brothers. I don't pull her, but I do keep a trained eye on her to make sure she doesn't run off in the other direction.

As we stumble quickly through the trees, my curiosity piques. "Vanessa, how did you end up here?"

She eyes me warily. "Demelza invited me." There's a moment's pause, but then the words pour out of her. "I didn't get out much at home, and she promised me it was safe here. I wanted to see it myself. And she was right. It's wonderful here. There are other

girls to talk with and freedom to explore. It's all I've ever wanted."
The twelve-year-old huffs gently as we run.

Her smile shows most of her teeth. Then it falters. "Jace is
mad, isn't he? I know I shouldn't have left without talking to my
brothers. But if I had told him, he never would have let me leave.
He would have argued it was too dangerous. But it's not! Demelza is
an amazing teacher and leader. She keeps everyone healthy and safe.
She's made us all a home here."

That is a lot of adoration for someone she barely knows.
Warning bells ring in my head. Nothing that good can be trusted.

Although I was starting to feel the same way about Jace
and his cabin. A person and a place providing escape. Newfound
freedom creating an illusion of security.

We finally reach them and I lean over, my hands on my knees,
gasping for breath. Vanessa slaps a hand over her mouth, horror
taking over her expression at the sight of Jace and Ian on the ground,
knees curled to their chests, rocking ever so slightly. Their hands
fist their hair. The pain has silenced them, turned them into shells.
Vanessa falls to her knees between them, reaching out to them.

"Jace, Ian." She sputters. They stir at the sound of her voice.

They struggle to talk, asking her questions. She answers
them tearfully.

I turn away.

My mind is on our next move. I recall the last time I escaped,
falling face first into the river. We can't drag them that far. And I'm
still not sure why we didn't enter Hazelgrove initially but landed
outside of the veil. Is it just because they are men? What has Demelza

done to this place? I don't want to risk anything worse happening to them. I hope it will be safer for them if we return beyond the veil before we leave. We still have the jar of water. Jace managed to hold on to it and replace the lid before our long walk. Once the horrible pain releases them, we can all decide where to go.

Layla's instructions ring in my mind.

I'm not ready to tell Jace. She had her threats, but if I can take them all with me to somewhere new, there's a chance she'll never reach us. And I really don't want to face Layla.

I wince.

I've ripped my hangnail open yet again.

"Let's get out of here." I spin on my heel to face the family. "We should leave before anyone comes looking." I pull the coat back onto my arms.

Jace looks at Vanessa. "Let's go home. You can explain everything there." His jaw still clenches as he tries to speak. I motion to Vanessa to help Jace, and I assist Ian. It takes everything we have, but we get them standing.

"Link hands." I shift Ian to be closest to the veil. Jace reaches out to me, keeping one hand on Vanessa's. She keeps turning to glance behind us. Longing shines in her eyes, and I can't tell if it's for her brothers or for the world we're taking her from.

Leaves rustle in the distance.

"Move now." I possess no desire to discover who made the sound.

"What are we doing?" Vanessa's voice pings with panic. Her brothers struggle to stay upright.

"We have to leave the woods first. Just walk with us. I'll show you."

She falls silent, brows drawn together. But she keeps hold of Jace's hand. Ian starts moving toward the light. He breaks through, pulling me after him. I follow, stepping forward. Jace's hand is firm in mine. We're going to do this. We'll make it out, and we'll make a plan.

As Jace moves through the curtain, I hear Vanessa whisper, "I'm sorry."

A crack of light blasts through the space next to me, electrifying and lightning quick.

I dive away from it onto the unforgiving sand. The trench coat saves my arms from taking a scraping. Behind me, a body thuds against the hard ground. I crane my neck to see.

No.

Jace's body splays out, his limbs taking on unnatural angles.

I rush to him, tripping over the rough ground, turning him over to see his face. His body is limp, with eyes shut. The acrid odor of singed flesh emanates from him. It takes everything in me not to freeze. I place my palm over his chest and feel it moving up and down.

He's breathing. He's unconscious, but he's still breathing.

I look up, and it's clear what happened. Vanessa didn't come with us. She's not here. Her unwillingness caused some problem with the veil. I don't know what it did to Jace, but I'm afraid to try passing through again. If she doesn't want to come, I can't force her.

"What's going on?" Ian falls to his knees next to us. He looks at his older brother, mouth hanging open. He jerks his head upward to survey the surroundings. He arrives at the same conclusion I did. And it breaks him. More tears fall down his face, this time accompanied by ragged sobs. He stares down the white wall of light in front of us, and I barely jump up in time to stop him from charging at it, shoving hard against his chest.

He trips backwards a few steps before coming to a stop. We look at each other, chests heaving, the unbearable heat closing in on us.

"You don't want to end up like that, do you?" I nod my head toward Jace.

"We came here for Vanessa, we found her, she needs to come home," he growls in my face.

"If she doesn't want to come, we can't change her mind now." Jace was right. He is always right. We should have done more research, prepared more.

But now we know Demelza has brainwashed their sister. She isn't lost and waiting for rescue. She wants to be here. She chose this. I'm not sure how we'll get her home now. If we will at all. I expect Ian to fight me, to blow past me and try going through the veil himself again. Instead, the fight slumps out of his shoulders.

"I just wanted to bring her home," he whispers.

I look at Jace, still unmoving on the ground. "Ian, grab the water." I can't help Vanessa, but I can still try to save Jace.

THIRTY-SEVEN

WE HUDDLE TOGETHER OVER Jace, holding tight to his arms. As Ian pours the last rivulet of water over my bloody nail bed, I send a silent plea for help.

Sophia, I need you.

We're instantly at the foot of her door, and I hear movement within the cottage. From my knees, I push against the heavy wood with my hand, and it swings open. Sophia has already set the table as a hospital bed. A clean white sheet drapes over the wood, and a stool full of jars and pouches sits at its side.

"Ian, take an arm. Sariah, you get the feet." Sophia says, appearing with a flourish of long skirts. She takes up the arm opposite Ian. "Steady." She instructs.

Together we hoist Jace up and carefully walk his body through the entryway, resting him on the table. She looks him over, her hands hovering in the air over his body. Her eyes pause to look at each of us, standing helplessly, waiting. "You both need rest. There are extra beds down the hall."

"I'm not going anywhere without my brother," Ian starts. One look from the woman withers his argument. He closes his mouth, but he doesn't move.

She continues her work with deft hands.

"Is he going to be okay?" I utter the question quietly, afraid to disturb the process.

"The wound is severe, but his spirit is strong. It will take time." She pulls his arm away from his torso to get a better look. I hadn't noticed it before, but the sight now makes me gasp. Angry red lines spread down the inside of his forearm, raised and blistering.

"That must be where he was hit." I recall the blinding flash of light.

Ian retreats now, backing up towards the hearth. He trips over a chair leg but manages to land in the seat. He slumps and holds his head in his hands.

The soft crackle of the fire calms the adrenaline racing through my veins. Exhaustion overtakes me. But I refuse to rest. I can do something. I can help.

I hear Sophia mutter under her breath. "Demelza, what has become of you?"

She gently swipes a salve over Jace's arm, but it doesn't close the skin the way it did for me.

"What's wrong?" I ask.

Sophia pauses. "Whatever portal you passed through was unusual. This wound is embedded deeper than the flesh. It is inside him."

I watch her step back to consider Jace's state, and the perplexed expression on her face twists my heart. She is the one with answers. With remedies. If she cannot assist him, it will be impossible for me to find him other help.

I want to vomit again. This is all my fault.

"What can I do?" The question strangles me. I pick at a new finger, my hands unable to keep still.

"He needs to remain here. I must observe him. He will need clothes. I—" She closes her mouth, then starts again. "I only own female attire. It will not fit him." She finishes quietly.

"I'll go." I look back at Ian behind me. He's still holding his head up, but his eyes have drifted closed. He could fall asleep any second. "Ian can stay here. I'll collect their things and bring them back."

Sophia nods. "Take great care, Sariah. The situation you have found yourselves in is pushing into realms that exceed your understanding. You must protect yourself now. Select those you trust prudently."

My mind runs over her words a few times, straining for clarity.

"Go now." She directs. "The sooner you can return, the better for your safety."

I hesitate, but shuffle to the door, watching Jace's chest rise and fall. I think another silent wish, this one to him.

Wake up.

I TAKE THE TREE-LINED path to the edge of the woods, then pause. Do I have to walk the entire distance to the cabin? It hadn't crossed my mind that I'd have no vehicle. Then a familiar white sedan approaches on the road. The driver rolls down his window.

John tips his hat to me. "Get in. I can drive you where you need to go."

I do as he says, the energy seeping out of me the longer I stand. "Thank you."

John doesn't ask questions as he drives. Trees flick past the window, casting their green blurs as apparitions flashing across my vision. Everything feels like an apparition now, my whole understanding of reality slipping like mist through my fingers. In a sense, I obtained what I've always longed for. An escape. Something other than the horrible repetitious life I was forced to live, that I've wished to leave. But is what I've found better?

One thing hasn't changed. I still don't know who I can trust.

When we get to the stretch of road closest to the cabin, John stops the car.

"I'll let you out here," he says softly. "I'll wait to take you back." He offers me a small smile before I exit. He has kind eyes. I hadn't noticed before.

"Thank you." I say again.

I climb out and trek through the grass and trees to the cabin.

It's so empty now. I pull the stolen trench coat tighter around me. My phone buzzes in the pocket. It startles me, but I quickly dig it out.

Layla. She doesn't waste any time, does she?

My thumb trembles over the button, but I know not answering is a significant risk. She knows so much more than I gave her credit for. For all I know, her guards could descend on me any second, and drag me into an interrogation. I force my thumb down, then hold the phone to my ear.

"Yes?" I breathe.

"Have you completed your first assignment?" Her tone now is so different than the frazzled assistant who warned me to run. Now it is clipped and polished. Strategic. Heartless.

I try to swallow, but my mouth has gone dry. "I found her, but—" I pause, my insides turning cold as I remember Vanessa's final words. "But she wouldn't come. She's still with Demelza."

The speaker crackles in her silence. After a moment, she replies. "And you have the object my guard delivered to you?"

Now I pause. What did I do with that box? The guard handed it to me, and I... I put it in my pocket. I shove a hand into the coat, but the box is gone. A surge of panic roils my gut.

"No." I whisper, then clear my throat. "No." I repeat louder. "I don't have it. I lost it."

"I see." Layla answers. "Well, if you wish to maintain your employ, I suggest you retrieve it as soon as possible." The line goes dead.

My head spins. I never opened the box. I don't know what was inside. Where would it have disappeared to? My hands start to shake. My torso goes tight. But I push against the panic. I can't fix the mistake now.

One breath. In. Out.

The inhale is shaky and weak.

The exhale sounds more like a sob.

Focus, Sariah. You are here for a reason.

I gather myself enough to walk to the elevator and click the buttons. It's so strange being here alone. After I exit at the bottom, I wait. With my luck, someone will appear out of the shadows. But there are no sounds. No hushed breath. No tiptoeing steps.

I am the only one here.

My feet carry me to the hallway, bypassing the room I've been sleeping in and stepping through Jace's door. I flip on the light and face the wall of sketches, letting my eyes roam over them all. My face plasters the space, as if this is where I always belonged.

One of the drawings catches my eye. I move forward and pull it from the others, gently tearing it from the small pin holding it to the wall. The picture depicts Jace and me standing close and looking at each other. Why does it seem so familiar?

I place the moment in my mind. It's a sketch of my first time coming here. When we were in the elevator. The ink is faded compared to the other drawings on the desk. I flip the page over and discover three words scribbled on the back.

She'll save us.

The sentence sends a strange mix of emotions through my chest.

What now?

THIRTY-EIGHT

Demelza

"SHHH, DON'T CRY." I stroke my fingers down Vanessa's long dark hair. "You were attacked, but you're safe now. You saved yourself, clever girl. I'm so glad you're here. We'll get you everything you need, understand?"

She is barely a woman, youth plump in her cheeks and evident in her small nose. But she's a special one. Not only does she bleed, but she dreams. Her blood isn't potent enough, not yet, but if she stays, I can keep testing.

She wipes her snot on her sleeve sheepishly, looking up at me from my lap. She was a mess when I found her, sobbing beside the veil. But I held her and talked her down, and now she smiles at me.

"Thank you, Demelza." Her blue eyes glitter, tears still stuck in her thick black lashes.

"Alta will take you home, get you to bed. You should rest now." A few women have been waiting for my signal. Alta emerges from the trees to welcome the girl. Vanessa has taken to her. Of course she has, a girl without a mother. She craves the love and warmth that emanate from our pregnant inhabitant.

Alta folds her into an embrace, then wraps an arm around her shoulders and guides her back to the settlement. I take a breath and stand, gently shaking the greenery from my skirt.

Sariah came back. And if Vanessa's report is true, she managed to bring two men with her. She is stronger than I gave her credit for. I should have run the test earlier. But she was so entrenched in Copeland's tactics, her brain was so clouded. I couldn't be sure she would return. Not voluntarily.

I must go immediately.

I walk back to the settlement, smiling at the volunteers milling about. So many happy women finally freed.

Before entering my own dwelling, I check that no one is behind me. No one is watching. Everyone seems content, so I open the door, and then lock it behind me. Rather than ascending to my rooms, I continue down the hall, to the farthest door.

This one looses a hiss when I pull it from the frame. The bright white lights click on, illuminating the stairs that lead me down, down, down, into the lab. My sanctuary of steel. At the bottom, I run my fingers across the long silver worktop.

I must not get my hopes up. She may not be the one. Just run the test, no expectations.

I open a drawer and pull out the vial. My nail clippings clink against the glass as I shake them out onto the table. I retrieve a microscope and position each nail to locate the blood. After she fell into the river, I knew I should save what little sample I managed to collect. There should be just enough.

Using a swab, I collect the blood from each nail clipping, then settle the cotton end into a sanitized dish. My heart beats faster within my ribs. After years of searching, the anticipation blooms against my restraint. From the refrigeration unit, I collect a small bottle of compound and set it next to the dish. My hands shake. I step back to gather myself.

It could be nothing. She may not be a match. But my heart won't listen to reason. I blow a measured breath through rounded lips. Willing my hands to still, I dip a dropper into the compound, sucking up exactly three drops.

Once I balance the dish under the microscope, I gingerly apply the three drops to the end of the swab. Then, I place my eye against the lens and wait.

One second.

Two seconds.

Three seconds.

The air catches in my throat, every other sense shutting down, my eye locked on the miracle erupting before me.

From where the compound and the blood soaked together, small steady growths branch off, filling the dish to its perimeter. The green lines are strong and bright. They look like veins.

Perfect.

She is a perfect match.

Dazed, I step back, bumping into the counter behind me.

Coming back to myself, I tear up the staircase and burst out the door. I must not attract attention to myself, so I slow my pace to a brisk walk, snaking back into the woods, past the river, and to the meadow.

Vanessa said Sariah dragged her into the tree line. I find the spot she occupied in the circle and then pace towards the edge of the meadow. My eyes scan the ground, looking for evidence of the struggle that allegedly occurred. I must corroborate the girl's story. If it is true that Sariah tried to take Vanessa from Hazelgrove, then I may be able to use the girl to my advantage. Use her to lure Sariah back here again.

There. Broken saplings and smashed grass, two long lines of upturned dirt where Vanessa must have dragged her feet.

But what is that?

A small, circular object glints up from the ground, next to an open box.

I ease myself onto my knees and pick the object up, holding it in my palm for inspection.

It can't be.

A laugh breaks loose from my lips. I allow myself a smile.

This may prove more fun than I imagined.

Acknowledgments

First and foremost, I must express my gratitude to God for entrusting me with this story and these characters, and for using this book to transform my life. I'm thankful to all the younger versions of myself that got me to this page. This book has been decades in the making, and despite my impatience, I know it has all culminated in perfect timing.

Thank you to my husband for supporting me on this publishing journey and cheering me on through late nights of working and stressing, through therapy and trauma recovery, through the everyday grind of parenthood, and for loving me every day. I would not be here without you.

To my daughters who will hopefully read this someday, thank you for your patience when mommy had to work and for being excited with me about my books. You both make me better and I love you forever.

An enormous thank you to Sara Carrington for your editorial work on the novella-version of this story. Your feedback gave me the nudge and the courage to develop it into a full-length novel. Thank you also for inducting me into our writing coven. Panera Ladies, I would not have made it to publication without your wisdom and support. Sara, Liz Johnson, Lindsay Harrel, Jennifer Deibel, Sarah Popovich, Erin McFarland, Ruth Douthitt, and Breana Johnson, your sisterhood and encouragement has blessed me so much.

Thank you to my beta readers for all of your notes, feedback, and excitement. Katie Conkel, my dearest sister, thank you for plowing through all the triggers and discussing with me the emotional impact of the book. You've been with me through it all. Karissa Ramirez, for all the workouts spent discussing my story and my business plan and my personal struggles, thank you, your friendship is irreplaceable. Sarah Popovich, your appreciation of Jace's character was hugely validating, thank you for your notes. Kelsy Moore, your insights were instrumental in nailing down the final edits of this book – thank you.

A huge shoutout to the designers at Miblart for bringing my cover concept to life so beautifully.

Thank you Rachel Badelita and our wonderful book club members for cheering me on through this writing process and for being my guinea pigs in the early phases of launching Water and Blood. And all my love goes out to the many friends who have followed up with me about how the book is going. Update: it's finally done!

I'd like to thank my therapist, who shall remain anonymous. You know who you are. Thank you for all your help and for getting me to the end of this book with my sanity intact, and my mental and emotional health in a much better place than where it started.

To my parents, thank you for all the books and all the movies and all the many tv shows. My love of story started at home.

And to my grandparents, thank you for all the other books. I've never been without reading material, and I count that as a huge blessing.

And perhaps most fervently, I wish to thank you, reader, for being here and sharing this piece of my soul. You've brought my own dreams to fruition. I hope you'll stick with me for the rest of this series and beyond.

LEAVE A REVIEW

I hope you enjoyed this book — if you did, please consider rating and reviewing it on your favorite platform. Your support goes a long way towards helping other readers discover my work as an indie author.

If you would like email updates about new releases, subscribe to my newsletter by visiting my website: kjwilkes.com

Your servant with a pen,

K.J. Wilkes

About the Author

K.J. Wilkes is a thriller and fantasy writer, known for her debut novel Water and Blood. When she's not writing, you can find her outdoors under a full moon, or in the kitchen tending her herbs and feeding her sourdough starter, Wanda. She resides near Phoenix, Arizona with her loving husband and two brilliant daughters.

kjwilkes.com
Instagram: @kjwilkes.author

www.ingramcontent.com/pod-product-compliance
Lightning Source LLC
Chambersburg PA
CBHW021005260626
47169CB00006B/1948